MADAM'S CREEK

BETSY REEDER

MADAM'S CREEK

BETSY REEDER

www. canterburyhousepublishing. com
Sarasota, Florida

Canterbury House Publishing

www. canterburyhousepublishing. com

Book Design by Tracy Arendt

Library of Congress Cataloging-in-Publication Data

Names: Reeder, Betsy, author.
Title: Madam's creek / Betsy Reeder.
Description: First edition. | Sarasota, Florida : Canterbury House
  Publishing, Ltd., [2017]
Identifiers: LCCN 2017029175 (print) | LCCN 2017039090 (ebook) | ISBN
  9781945401015 | ISBN 9781945401008 (softcover)
Subjects: | GSAFD: Love stories.
Classification: LCC PS3618.E43595 (ebook) | LCC PS3618.E43595 M36 2017
  (print) | DDC 813/.6--dc23
LC record available at https://lccn.loc.gov/2017029175

First Edition: October 2017

Author's Note:
This is a work of fiction. Although an effort was made to use surnames
and geographic identities of the area in the mid-nineteenth century, names,
characters, places, and incidents are either the products of the author's
imagination or are used fictitiously. Exceptions are members of the Richmond
and Bennett families, as well as a few historic figures—including Captain
Philip Thurmond—and military engagements of the Civil War. Otherwise, any
resemblance to actual persons living or dead, business establishments, events,
or locales is entirely coincidental.

DEDICATION

With boundless love, this book is dedicated to Dad, who encouraged me by his example to be creative; to Mom, who encouraged me to write; and to Jessie, who mirrors her grandparents in her loving support and reminds me every day that I am blessed beyond measure.

MAP

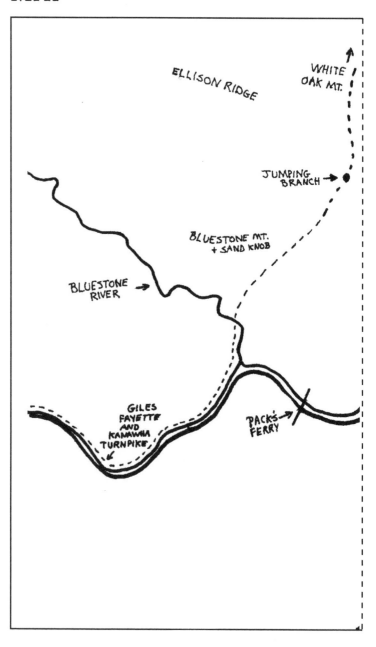

NORTH →

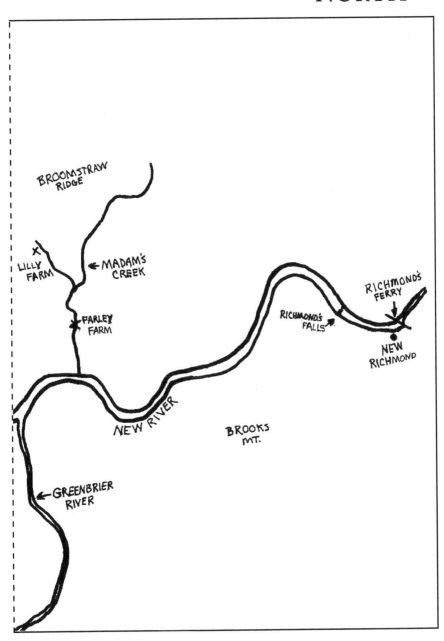

CHAPTER ONE

It could have been a happy time that spring. The mountainsides wore a blush of pastels as buds burst open. Grasses along roadsides and riverbanks grew thick in a tumult of fecund green. Mayflies lifted off the river, attracting hundreds of swallows that swooped and darted inches above the choppy surface. Maylene's baby, with a head of hair the color of raven wings, toddled unsteadily about, plucking dandelions.

The final echo of deafening artillery had faded—at long last—to silence, the smoke of gunpowder dispersed. The horrendous war was over.

It could have been such a happy time.

FOURTEEN YEARS EARLIER

The barefoot, shirtless boy crouched by a mountain stream, his head down, tawny hair fallen across one eye. He was putting the finishing touches on a ten-inch tower made of small, flat stones, still dark with water, glistening in sunlight that dappled them and the tanned hands that placed them. Next to the boy was a blond, freckled girl of similar size on all fours, her dress wet nearly to her waist. She busied herself constructing a roof of bark on a little stone house. Its chimney-tower complete, the boy stood up to study his handiwork.

"He was at the Hintons' place last night," said the boy. "That's where he got the shingles."

"Did the rocks come from our chimney again?"

"Some of 'em did."

"Which is the next cabin to fall? I'm thinking the Hintons' is close to collapse."

"Uh-huh, but the stallion shall warn the children tonight. He shall carry them away if they trust him."

"I would trust him."

"But you *know*."

"Even if I didn't, I'd trust him."

The boy spotted and pounced on something. "Here. This little rock can be the door."

"I think the Hooded Thief is foolish to keep building next to the creek and having his houses wash away."

"But if he didn't, he'd have no reason to keep stealing."

"Why does he want to steal?"

"I don't know, but he wouldn't be the Hooded Thief if he didn't."

"Will you draw him?"

"Sure."

The boy picked up a fallen birch branch and broke it across his knee. With a pointed end he began sketching in soft silt next to the water's edge—beneath a pointed hood appeared an oblong face with squinty eyes, a beaked nose, and a lipless mouth.

"He looks mean," said the girl.

"Good," said the boy. "He is."

Maylene Farley was the third of four girls. The boy, Robert, Jr., who they called Robin, was the youngest and the apple of their papa's eye. He got a fever and died a week shy of his third birthday. They buried him under a thorn tree at the back edge of the little family plot, and Papa never spoke of him again. It was

Maylene and her sister Mary who picked daisies in June and took them up the steep, rocky path into the high woods, to the marker Papa carried there on his own back. It was Maylene who remembered the day of Robin's passing, the ninth of March, etched indelibly on her eight-year-old mind as she watched her father scratching at the sandstone slab he'd chosen. But even Mama didn't mark the date. It was only Maylene who visited the little grave in early March if the snow wasn't too deep, as it was the year she turned ten. And she did so furtively, as if she were in the wrong.

The girls grew up strong and wild, filling in as surrogate sons as best they could. There was little choice in the matter—Papa needed help in the fields, and it required the entire family to tend the garden. Demands for manual labor proliferated faster than weeds on the narrow farm that flanked both sides of Madam's Creek. Maylene gravitated more than the others to the outdoor chores, which offered the benefit of her father's quiet company. Despite complaints, however, Mary and Melva often joined Maylene planting crops, cutting hay and grain, binding sheaves, threshing wheat and oats, shelling corn, picking apples, and tending livestock, while Margaret was too small to do much more than gather eggs and fistfuls of dandelion greens.

Papa drew the line at certain tasks, though. He alone did the plowing with their mules, Dolly and Spit (Spit, short for Spitfire, an unruly colt who tried Papa's patience sorely in the training years). He alone did the smithing at his anvil in a lean-to adjacent the barn. And he never allowed his daughters to accompany him to repair the washed-out road, typically in spring, when farmers and their sons labored from dawn to dusk with mattocks and picks to fill in the worst ruts and remove boulders that tumbled down the mountainside, launched by thaws and downpours. Their efforts went only as far as Charlton's Mill, a fifteen-minute wagon ride above the Farley farm. The condition of the road beyond the mill—where it began to climb in earnest—was of little concern to those downstream. On their own lane, the spur that came off the Madam's Creek road, Papa sometimes enlisted his daughters' help. And while Bob Farley alone split rails, his daughters one after the other became handy with an axe and adept at splitting firewood. Their mother, Sara Mae, swung an axe like a lumberjack.

Sara Mae, too, insisted on certain appearances. In the warmer months, after their Saturday night baths in the washtub, the Farley family was the picture of respectability setting out for church with four barefoot girls in bonnets and faded but clean gingham dresses that hid their boyish muscles. Mary, Melva, Maylene, and little Margaret. Mary was given the name of her deceased paternal grandmother. Melva was named after Sara Mae's younger brother Melvin who had died of appendicitis at age fourteen. Maylene was named after Sara Mae, and Margaret was offered a name starting with M so she wouldn't feel left out. All blond, blue-eyed, and more or less freckled, with wide, honest faces. The Farleys' "mountain wagon" creaked and complained its way down Madam's Creek to the white-washed log church perched above the rush of water hell-bent for New River a quarter-mile below.

Most often Maylene couldn't remember more than the opening sentences of a sermon, those forty or fifty minutes being devoted to a fantasy life that might involve anything from adoption of a pet bear cub, to pursuit through the woods by an ill-defined agent of the Devil, to bareback races on a magnificent gray thoroughbred. Only the hymns roused her from her daydreams, pulling her back to the hard bench and Pastor Mullens' nasal yet soothing voice. She sang with gusto.

It was a pleasure to be released at the end of the service, when the girls scrambled into the wagon's short bed, jostling for position on the straw-covered floor. In the colder weather, they burrowed under a quilt, giggling and squirming, making sure to shove their feet under as much straw as they could for the ride back up the "holler." Margaret invariably ended up on a lap, baby that she was. Maylene preferred her on someone else's.

Papa would say hup, hup to get the mule team moving. Then Maylene liked to settle herself flat and watch the branches overhead. In their winter nakedness, they scratched at the sky like eager pencils, quick and sure, and made the old wagon seem to be moving faster than it was. Maylene imagined hemlock boughs as paintbrush tips smearing the sky with white streamers or splashing fist-shaped clouds against the blue. The trip home took less than a half hour, that's what Mama said, but it was usually long enough to wrap up whatever delicious escapade had begun during the sermon. Maylene had long since learned to shut out the chatter of three siblings.

When the mules turned in at the Farley farm, quickened their pace, and made their noisy way across the bridge spanning the creek, Maylene turned her attention to the best offering of the Lord's Day—there was a strong chance Marcus would show up.

On a gilded fall day, the Lilly boys headed upstream for home when they left their one-room schoolhouse, opposite the direction of Maylene and her older sisters. The tallest boy made sure to lead the way, setting a heart-pounding pace that alternated between walking and running. For amusement, the boys picked up small stones during their walking spells, and took aim at tree trunks.

The red-haired tallest said, "I'll bet you can't hit that sourwood yonder," and let his own pebble fly. It struck beneath the umbrella of scarlet leaves, squarely in the trunk's center. A flake of bark burst skyward, landing after the stone.

The other redhead fired and missed.

"Just as I said," came the critique.

"Who says I was aimin' for that one?" said the put-down boy.

The boy with hair the color of a buckskin, stooping for ammunition, was distracted by a streak of bright orange no longer and scarcely wider than a leaf stem. He pushed away a slender, moss-covered log, already knowing what he would find, a red eft. With a gentle grasp, he lifted the vividly colored amphibian and placed it in one palm to examine its red spots ringed with black. He felt its cool dry skin on his own, its sticky little toes, splayed as if reaching for its lost world. He looked into the black, unblinking eyes.

"Hi."

His older brother had stopped and stood impatiently tossing and catching a small stone.

"What you got now, Marcus?"

"Just a salamander."

"Let me see it." The taller boy moved in Marcus's direction.

"No!" Marcus returned the eft to the far side of the mossy log and began to run, as fast as his legs would carry him, toward home.

He knew Junior—unwilling to be beaten in a foot race— would give chase, and give chase he did. As he passed Marcus, he thrust out an arm and shoved him off the rough path.

Marcus nearly fell, then returned to a walk. Let Johnny continue the pointless race. Marcus was satisfied he had won his goal.

Marcus Lilly wasn't like the other boys, rowdy and loud. He kept to himself a good bit, despite having four brothers and an equal number of sisters. He was second in line, close on the heels of Quentin Junior and scarcely older than Johnny. Then came the four girls, after which his parents had taken a pause before producing two more sons.

Quentin Senior liked hearing he was one of the richest men in Raleigh County, but it was a nod to his luck not wealth, of which there was none. Quentin and Suzanne Lilly were rich in children, as not one had died of fever, and they all seemed uncommonly immune to the usual mishaps of childhood. Not a broken bone or ankle sprain and it was rare even for one of them to catch cold. Quentin didn't hesitate to take credit.

The Lilly farm was high above Madam's Creek, nearly halfway up the mountain to the crest of Broomstraw Ridge. It sat in a sort of tilted bowl, where a little run came wandering down looking for the larger creek. The flatter part held a sprawling garden, a barn, a pig sty, a smoke house, a chicken coop, a small paddock, a smaller pond, and a two-story log house. Corn, wheat, oats, flax, and hay grew on surrounding slopes, with steeper terrain beyond reserved for grazing. The pastures were stubbly—it hadn't been so long since the land was cleared, and the largest stumps remained. Quentin's pa had come over from Sand Knob and done the work with his sons. But Jake Lilly was dead now, resting up at the top of the pasture with his wife Ellie. Quentin's five sisters had been married off, and the two brothers had moved on. Only Quentin remained on the family farm, with Suzanne and their nine shockingly healthy offspring.

Marcus strongly resembled his mother with his sandy hair, narrow face, pointed chin, and light build. Only his eyes differed—they were brown instead of blue, slightly darker than his father's. Junior and Johnny looked more like their round-faced, red-and-unruly-headed pa, carrying more bulk and height.

Marcus was undeniably different. His mother took note, but not the rest. In a family of eleven, one was bound to be a trifle of his own making. The boy had a shy gracefulness, like a deer that moves while making as little noise as possible. He hung back, watching. Yet he was impish, quick to smile, not a brooding child.

One of his hallmarks was a passion for reading. As soon as he learned his letters at the schoolhouse, he had a new zest for his chores. At the end of a summer day, once he'd gotten his garden section free of weeds, the chickens secured for the night, and firewood carried in for the morning fire, Marcus would head for the porch steps in failing light with the family's lone book—a weary-looking, leather-bound Bible. No amount of teasing—and he got plenty from Junior and Johnny—could keep him from the printed Word.

Second only to reading was Marcus's love of drawing. He would sketch with a lump of charcoal on a porch plank or with a sharpened stick in mud by the creek if he didn't have pencil and paper, which he commonly didn't. His brothers and sisters became used to finding a rearing stallion or an oversized snapping turtle scratched into the flat places where silt piled up after heavy rains. A human face on the porch rail. What was invisible to them were the dramas played out in Marcus's mind, stories he illustrated with carbon or broken branch.

Only Maylene was granted entry to Marcus's fantasy life. They were close in age and gravitated naturally to each other when the Lilly and Farley children went wandering.

It was not purely for pleasure that the children took to the woods—there was food there. Spring was the season for digging ramps, their potent, oniony stench on the breath of every child at the schoolhouse for weeks. It was also the season for morels, oval mushrooms reminiscent of small brains pushing up through last year's leaves, fried in butter to the delight of Maylene in particular. It was the season for fiddleheads, the coiled and tender shoots of emerging ferns. Come summer, wild cherries ripened, followed by the appearance of elderberries. Next in line were blackberries all along the pasture and road edges, their thorns inadequate defense against packs of hungry youngsters. Sometimes Maylene and Marcus, along with a sibling or two, would go all the way up to a rocky bald on Broomstraw Ridge to gather blueberries, if bears and birds didn't beat them to it. Later, there were pawpaws down along Madam's Creek. Fall brought chestnuts, walnuts, and butternuts by the bushel-basket. And Marcus had a knack for knowing just where and when to find ripe persimmons, sweet and plump, hanging like miniature pumpkins for the taking. He and Maylene liked to climb for them, although there were always many scattered on the ground.

In addition to gathering foods of various sorts, the children fished. It wasn't far to New River, down the rock-strewn, rut-gouged road that hugged the west bank of Madam's Creek. Stern warnings accompanied the young anglers—New River, called "River of Death" by the Indians, was not to be taken lightly. Even at its shallowest summer flows it carried a strong current, its bed pocked with holes of swirling water that could trap an unsuspecting child. The commandment was to fish from the bank, and Maylene and the others had heard enough cautionary tales to obey.

What stuck in Maylene's head was the memory of a drowned calf. She hadn't been much more than a toddler when Papa took her and her two older sisters down to the river to watch the spectacle of spring runoff. Snow pack from the highlands became a torrent of muddy water every March, and it was a sight to behold as it spiraled and churned its way toward the Ohio. The calf had passed close to the bank. Maylene could still picture its slow spinning in the fast-moving water, its blind, staring eye. She had reached for Mary's hand.

She was content to stay out of the water. Agile as squirrels, the children perched on sycamore roots, dropping a crawdad or hellgrammite into the quieter spots. Even Margaret knew to suppress her shouts of excitement when a line was struck. Fishing required a reverential hush.

Proud and sun-blushed, the Farley and Lilly children straggled home under loads of catfish, chubs, and suckers, their way shaded by leaves and striped by tree-trunk shadows as the sun sank.

While they fished or scoured the woods, Marcus would tell his stories to Maylene, who listened with rapt attention and asked many questions. He fell quiet when the others came within earshot, however, guarding the output of his imagination. Often Maylene modified his flights of fancy, adding characters and twists to the plots. These changes didn't offend Marcus in the least but added grist to the mill of his busy mind.

When the day's end interrupted a particularly rich fantasy, the duo would vow to remember where they left off. Even if they didn't see each other again for weeks, they would recall precisely where in the drama they had paused, and pick it up again.

Maylene sometimes asked Marcus to draw a villain or creature for her, and he would sweep away twigs and leaves to create a canvas of forest soil, or pluck angular sandstone fragments out of sandy mud along the river to clear a spot. The images were cartoonish, yet strangely expressive. Of special interest were images of terror, including the giant bat that snatched children at dusk, or the salivating bear that tracked children through the woods on silent paws, and even oversized snails with bizarrely extendable, toxic tentacles. Their favorite, however, was the Hooded Thief, who disassembled homes a sliver of log, a shingle, a morsel of mortar at a time. If his misdeeds went undetected too long, an entire home would collapse on an unsuspecting family, always at night.

One day, as Marcus recounted the latest mischief of the Hooded Thief, Maylene concocted a battle involving Marcus and a slingshot, in the fashion of David slaying Goliath. She pronounced victory when one of the slung stones struck the Hooded Thief in an eye. From that time forward, Marcus drew the villain with an X in place of one eye.

CHAPTER TWO

Their most memorable outing was a fishing trip on a fine spring afternoon. It was the first day warm enough for shirtsleeves, and it fell on a Sunday. Maylene and Marcus hatched their plan at church, making certain their siblings didn't overhear. This was to be a day all their own.

After a leisurely dinner that took up too much time, Maylene waited impatiently on the porch—homemade fishing rod in hand—for Marcus to arrive. It was downhill the entire way from the Lilly's farm to the Farley's, and Marcus ran the whole route, winding down the path along the nameless stream until it met Madam's Creek, at which point the path became a dirt road. With the practice of years, his feet found the flat spots between ruts and rocks, and he navigated the rough road with the ease of a loping hound.

He arrived out of breath. "Ready?"

"Let's go!" Maylene sprinted toward the bridge, with Marcus on her heels.

"Slow down. I ain't caught my breath yet," he struggled to get out.

"I'll wait for you at the river."

Marcus could see the pale soles of Maylene's feet flashing as she flew in the direction of the New, the wind whipping her green dress like the mane of a galloping horse. She disappeared beyond a gauze of lavender. Dozens of redbuds in bloom along Madam's Creek.

The fish weren't biting at the usual spot, so the children moved downstream to try another, and then another. At their fifth location, they began at last to feel nibbles on their lines and settled, squatting, on a flat rock outcrop with the breathless anticipation of success. The water, deep and translucent-green, drew their baits downstream with the muscle of spring runoff, forcing them to support their makeshift poles with two-fisted grasps. Each hoped to outdo the other, competition coming naturally to their pursuit. The sun, however, proved traitorous. It stranded them like castaways as clouds obscured it, and the wind picked up strength.

"Are you cold?" asked Marcus, not wanting to be the first to say he was getting goose bumps.

"I'm getting there. Look."

Inky clouds were boiling over Swell Mountain, which loomed behind them. A storm was coming. And fast.

"We'd best get back." That was Marcus.

Maylene gathered the short line and wrapped it around her pole. She turned and stepped down from the platform rock onto a lower slab, which looked perfectly trustworthy but had been undercut by high spring flows. Her weight was all the persuasion it needed to tip toward the water like a seesaw abandoned at one end. Maylene gasped as it fell away. She pinwheeled her arms in a desperate attempt to save herself, but her momentum committed her to the wayward rock. She cried out as she felt herself plummeting toward the waiting water, the water of the river she was never, ever to enter.

Her head went entirely under the still-frigid water, and the shock of it struck like a thunderclap. Maylene felt the current pulling her, sucking her downstream. Although strong for her size, her small arms were no match for that terrifying tugging. She felt she was being drawn down the throat of an icy snake and a ferocious, fighting panic rose in her. Her feet found the bottom and she threw her head and shoulders out, but a thin slime of algae on the rocks prevented a foothold. She scrabbled and slipped and went under again.

She banged a knee hard on a rock, shoved a heel down, and got her head out a second time, then lost her footing again and started to submerge when she felt a hand on her arm. Like a fish at the end of a line, she stopped moving downstream. She was being reeled in, toward the bank, which was no more than an arm's length away.

Beloved Marcus. With his hand to steady her, she was able to climb out.

"Are you all right?"

"I think so."

But Maylene's teeth were already chattering, and her lips had a blue tinge. Marcus, who had gotten wet only to his thighs, removed his shirt at once.

"Here, put this on."

Maylene found her hands so clumsy Marcus had to help her. As her dripping hair immediately began to darken the shoulders and back of the shirt, Marcus gathered a fistful of sodden locks and wrung out water, water the wind snatched and scattered.

"Sorry. Should have done this first," he said more to himself than to Maylene.

By now the wind was vicious, the sky dark as twilight. Neither child had to be prompted to run.

Within seconds, hail began to pummel them. They scanned the mountainside for a large leaning trunk.

"There!" Maylene yelled, and they dashed under the protective ceiling of a toppled tulip poplar. Caught in the crotch of another tree, the wide trunk offered instant relief from a punishing pelting by pea-sized balls of ice.

Although Marcus had been somewhat warmed by their brief sprint, Maylene had not. She dropped to a crouch, hugging her knees. Her shivering was violent. To the din of hail slapping the river and stinging overhead branches, Marcus went to work.

"Give me your hands."

He vigorously rubbed Maylene's icy fingers between his palms. He moved on to her arms, then her chilled feet. His efforts warmed him more than her, however. Maylene continued to shiver uncontrollably. Marcus was sure the temperature had dropped at least fifteen degrees, and the wind made it feel far worse than that.

In minutes, the ice pellets turned to heavy rain. There was nothing to do but wait it out despite the inadequacy of their shelter, which had held off the hail fairly well but wasn't much of a stronghold against wind-driven rain. Marcus tried to distract Maylene with conversation, but she seemed incapable of forcing words past her chattering teeth. He moved to where he had more overhead clearance and started jumping up and down. He was missing his shirt and starting to shiver himself.

"Come up here and jump with me. It helps."

"In a m-minute."

But Maylene didn't move, and Marcus soon returned to her. He bent over and rubbed his hands up and down on either side of her spine.

"Does that help?"

"Uh-huh," Maylene lied.

Marcus squatted next to her, hoping his body heat would reach her. Feeling hesitant, he put an arm around her shoulders. Maylene's shaking alarmed him—her entire body was wracked by wave upon wave of wretched quaking.

The rain began tapering off. Marcus said, "Let's get out of here. You're freezing."

He stepped out from under the fallen poplar, but Maylene didn't follow. "Are you coming?"

Maylene didn't answer but continued to huddle and shiver as if he hadn't spoken.

"Come on! We'll run. It will warm you."

No reply.

Marcus was dumbfounded. What was wrong with her?

He raised his voice. "Come on! We're going home now!"

Maylene looked up at him. Her expression was dazed and uncomprehending.

Marcus ducked back under the trunk and put his face close to Maylene's. "Listen to me. Listen! The Hooded Thief has been to this home. It's ready to fall. The timbers are cracking. Do you hear? The stallion is here to warn us. We have to run! Now! Come, Maylene!"

Marcus didn't know if it was his words or the urgency in his voice, but something reached her. Maylene got to her feet and Marcus took her hand. He pulled and she ran, slowly and clumsily, but she ran.

They were nearly two miles from the Farley farm, and it was slow going. Maylene stopped repeatedly and had to be urged along. But she was coming back to life, losing the blue in her lips and fingernails.

Halfway home, Mary appeared on Dolly, sent by Papa who was concerned by the change in the sky, although there had been no more than light rain at home. Mary wrapped her sister in a wool blanket and insisted Maylene walk, not ride, the rest of the way. Maylene made no protest. She remained chilled to the bone and had revived enough to crave exertion. A grateful Marcus accepted the second blanket, which he folded in half and tied, cape-like, around his neck. The Sun was out again, though with less vigor, helping ease his own chill.

At the sight of her drenched daughter, a fretful Sara Mae fired the stove and put on a pan of milk to scald. Maylene seared her tongue in her thirst for warmth, but was soon herself again, with her only sign of injury a bruised and swollen knee. She said only that she had fallen. Neither she nor Marcus ever said a word about her plunge into the River of Death, and Mary kept to herself her observation that Maylene had returned home without her fishing pole.

CHAPTER THREE

Puberty could have ruined the friendship. Marcus and Maylene were too comfortable in each other's company to flinch at the siren call of hormones, however. It was effortless to pretend nothing had changed, at first. As their fantasies began to feel childish, they replaced them with discussions of their surroundings. Marcus pointed out bobcat tracks along the creek. Maylene said she knew of a den site above their back pasture. Marcus was alert to meadowlarks staking out territories in the Lilly hayfield and made haste to the Farley farm with the news, suggesting it wasn't too early to scout for ramps. He would relate the secrets of his success as a gobbler hunter. Maylene had her own theories of turkey psychology, and they practiced their imitative calls. They collected honeysuckle and sat on the Farley porch, weaving baskets.

Between the two of them, Maylene and Marcus held extensive knowledge of the terrain, the seasonal changes, and the living things that had enchanted and nourished them all their years. They delighted in sharing and expanding that knowledge, and they remained inseparable.

Naturally, their parents and siblings assumed they would marry. It was impossible to imagine either of them with any other partner—they simply belonged together, like the two halves of a walnut shell.

Junior would sometimes tease Marcus, saying, "Have you named all the young'uns yet or just the oldest?"

Marcus would punch his brother's arm and a bout of wrestling would invariably ensue, with Marcus the loser.

One thing in particular had changed, however. Maylene had transformed from a sweet-faced girl into a striking teen with an enviable figure and silky, waist-length hair suggestive of a sunlit wheatfield. Unbeknownst to her, she was turning heads.

It wasn't often that she accompanied her father out of their holler, her typical outings being to the river, the Baptist church, the Lilly farm, and much of the rugged, wooded land that lay between those destinations. But on occasion she tagged along on half-day trips up New River to Pack's Ferry near the mouth of Bluestone River or all-day trips to the village of Jumping Branch, accessed by going up the Bluestone a short distance to pick up the newly completed Giles, Fayette, and Kanawha Turnpike, an honest-to-goodness, wagon-worthy road. This route went up Bluestone Mountain and then across several rolling miles to where Broomstraw Ridge terminated at the shallow valley of a stream by said name, Jumping Branch. The small community there boasted a general store, the closest one to Madam's Creek. There was a far shorter way by foot or horseback, which passed the Lilly farm, as well as a wagon road that climbed Broomstraw Ridge on its way west, but for the sake of his wagon and mules, Bob preferred the Turnpike. This meant taking the circuitous route that occupied an entire day, round-trip.

Meador's Store—where mail was retrieved, where sugar and spices were purchased in the rare event they could be afforded, where newspapers found their way from Lynchburg and Richmond—held special appeal for Maylene because it offered the possibility of a package. Her mother's parents, who lived in Charlottesville, had given up on homesteading in the wilds of Raleigh County years before Maylene's birth and retreated east shortly after their son Melvin's tragic death. They had taken along their surviving children save Sara Mae, who by then was betrothed to a childless widower named Bob Farley. Maylene's grandpa, with his bird-legged, meager-muscled physique, was better suited for handling a ledger than a plow anyhow. He worked as a banker and had some money, just enough that a novel was sent from time to time, a little worn from the handling of Grandma, several aunts, and one uncle.

Last year's selection was the first volume of Harriet Beecher Stowe's *Dred: A Tale of the Great Dismal Swamp*, passed on like all the rest to Marcus once the Farley girls had had their fill. As the best reader in his family, Marcus read to his eight siblings in the evenings, before bed. Greedily, he read ahead as well. Even when milking the cow, he was known to use a slower, one-handed method, as he balanced precariously on the stool, book in hand, with scarcely enough dawn or dusk light to make out the words.

"Can't you wait for Sunday?" his pa would ask, shaking his head.

It was on one such trip to the Jumping Branch store that Maylene caught the attention of Amos Wallace. At nineteen, Amos was several years older than Maylene. He lived on a hard-luck farm on Broomstraw Ridge, where the fields grew more rocks and thorns than crops. The sullen-looking Wallace children were skinny as asparagus stalks, and some had died. They kept apart.

Amos, however, cleaned up and came to church, less interested in avoiding eternal damnation than in seeing Maylene again. He was dark-haired, hazel-eyed, tall and lean and rather handsome. The Lilly girls took notice, even the youngest. Maylene recognized him at once.

Amos wasted no time speaking to Maylene after the service, when she would normally have sought out Marcus.

"Nice to see you again, Miss Farley. That's a right pretty dress. Did you make it yourself?"

Maylene was mortified to feel herself blush. She saw Marcus glance at her as he passed without a word.

"I did. It's only an old thing."

"Well you sure do dress it up. I hope I'll have the pleasure of seeing you in it again next week."

With that, Amos nodded, ever so slightly, letting his gaze take in Maylene's form from top to bottom and back again. A half smile tugged at his lips, as if he were privy to a secret. Maylene felt simultaneous alarm and excitement, aware of both the offensiveness and the titillation of that bold appraisal. There was nothing casual about it—it was charged with expectation.

Amos turned for his waiting horse, leaving Maylene in a buzzy haze that felt, well, better than nearly anything.

Maylene fretted over her hair the next Sunday, trying to smooth it against the dampness of mist—the perpetual fog of Indian-summer mornings—rising up the flank of the mountain from the New. Her blue dress felt plain and worn. How had she not noticed before? She practiced folding the skirt over a faint gravy stain on the hem.

Maylene scanned the small sanctuary three times before Pastor Mullens took his place behind a podium of knotty pine and laid open his Bible.

Amos wasn't there.

It was during the first hymn that he arrived, easing into place on a back bench. Maylene noticed the surge of light when the door opened, and sneaked a look. To her regret, she caught Marcus's eye—two benches back and across the aisle with his overflowing family—as she turned back.

Maylene listened for Amos's voice to join in but couldn't pick it out, then realized Amos was unlikely to know the words. The rest of the service was incomprehensible. All she knew was that Amos Wallace sat and stood behind her, his eyes upon her. She could feel his gaze like the itch of a gnat bite.

Maylene feigned surprise when he came up behind her as she made her way to the wagon.

"Now don't you go sneakin' off, Miss Maylene," Amos said.

Maylene liked the less-formal address.

"Don't you go depriving me of a word with the prettiest girl on Madam's Creek," he continued with a trace of a whine.

"It's nice to see you again." Maylene caught herself in time to prevent a curtsey. She gathered her skirt with one hand and swung it, with a demure flip of her wrist, over the stain. As she could think of nothing further to say, she was grateful Amos filled the gap like a dog snatching up a bone.

"Now you tell me, Miss Maylene, just how many suitors do you have? I can't imagine I'm the only man who has taken a fancy. If I were to pay you a visit some Sunday afternoon, how many would I have to fight off with a stick?"

She was blushing again. This was not a man to beat around the bush. Maylene admired that.

"There's not very many."

"How many is that?"

Maylene hesitated. She didn't want to lie, or tell the truth either.

"No more than one." She was thinking of Marcus. Was he a suitor? He didn't act like one.

"Then I'm in luck! I can take him with one arm tied behind my back." Amos laughed, and Maylene couldn't help laughing, too, although she didn't like to imagine Amos "taking" Marcus. Although far from timid, Marcus was no fighter, at least she didn't think so.

"Miss Maylene, do me the honor of asking your daddy if I may escort you home from church next Sunday." It was more of a command than a request.

"All right."

"That's my girl." Amos winked and walked away.

Bob Farley bristled. "That boy should have asked me himself."

"I know, but you were busy talking with Mr. Adkins. I think he was hesitant to interrupt," Maylene lied, immediately ashamed.

"Well, I don't suppose there's harm in a ride home from church, but tell Amos I expect him to stay and visit with the family at dinner."

"I'm sure he'll like that. Thank you, Papa."

Maylene could understand how hard it was for her father to see his daughters go. Mary was already married and had moved down New River, all the way to New Richmond. She was expecting a baby in the winter. Papa could take comfort in Melva, however, who was likely to be home awhile longer. She looked much like Maylene, but taller, with a slimmer build and fewer freckles. Her strawberry-blond hair had a natural waviness Maylene coveted. But Melva spoke with a lisp and was shy as a stray cat. She avoided associating with strangers and had never been friendly with the boys at school. If Amos had come to church seeking her, he would have been lucky to get as much as eye contact. Maylene figured only the loneliness of having all her sisters gone could compel Melva to become receptive to a man, and he would have to be a patient one.

Maylene slept very little that Saturday night. This was nothing like having Marcus over. Putting an extra plate out for him felt as casual as the two added plates for Mary's and Corbin's visits. Amos was courting her, and making no bones about it. This was a dizzying reality that had broken like a great, cresting wave over her predictable, flatwater world. What do you say to a man who flatters you and devours you with his eyes? How do you deflect him long enough to find out who he is?

Marcus was wretched. His brothers didn't help.

"Maylene and Amos," sang Junior.

"Will you challenge him to a duel?" Johnny asked.

"Fools! You don't know anything. I've got no claim on Maylene," said Marcus, storming out of the house.

He retreated to the woods, and found himself climbing all the way up to the ridgetop. He arrived, winded, at the rocky outcrop where he and Maylene gathered blueberries. There he sat, fuming, whittling a locust stick.

He hadn't been able to shut out Amos's voice. Did you make it yourself? Well you sure do dress it up.

He shot back, No, Amos, her maid made it. Who do you think? Dress it up? Maylene would look pretty in a pile of rags. Why state the obvious? Are you dim?

Marcus couldn't imagine telling Maylene she looked pretty. It made about as much sense as telling her the days were getting shorter and winter was coming.

He sent long strips of wood flying. No recognizable form was taking shape.

Marcus had never had to compete for Maylene. Even wise-cracking Junior had never made a move in her direction. Johnny was probably tempted but knew Maylene had no interest in him. Amos felt like a dire threat—taller, older, and Marcus assumed, by anyone's criteria, better looking. Worst of all, he was smooth talking. Marcus feared he'd treated Maylene like a sister for too long. How was he going to learn sweet-talk overnight? It was far easier to picture Maylene laughing at him than falling into his arms if he began talking like Amos.

And when was he going to see her if Amos began monopolizing her Sundays? At thirteen, Maylene and Marcus had graduated from the Madam's Creek School, situated between their homes, near the mill. The Sabbath was their sole remaining point of contact.

Marcus was not accustomed to either fear or powerlessness. He could remember only one time he had felt their combined power—the day Maylene had fallen into the river. He had thrown himself across their sandstone perch, onto his chest, but missed on his first attempt to grab her, his hand closing on air and splashing water as the current carried her away. With a sickening sense of desperation, he made the leap of a lifetime, a downstream leap off the rock shelf, a leap of athleticism inspired by unmitigated terror. He seemed suspended in air, landing in slow motion, with time to plant his feet between the rough stones that could have toppled him. He then plunged into the water, holding the lifeline of a tree branch with one hand, reaching for Maylene with the other. The turbulent water carried her to him. The feel of her forearm in his grip allowed time to return to its normal pace. He had her. He would not let her go until she was standing next to him, and he did not.

That night he had lain awake unable to fight off the what-ifs. He'd told himself Maylene wouldn't have drowned if he hadn't reached her. She knew how to swim and would have overcome her panic, stopped trying to stand in the impossible current on the hopelessly slippery rocks, and simply swum to safety. But he wasn't sure. Even at age eleven, it was easy for a child with his vivid imagination to visualize what could have happened. His mind replayed the image of Maylene's golden hair swept across her face, her green dress swirling. She had seemed to be becoming part of the river and he'd felt powerless to stop it from claiming her. He could see himself pulling her free of a logjam, laying her out like a shot muskrat on the bank, dragging himself to the Farleys' door, forcing his lungs and throat and tongue to form the hideous words, "Maylene is dead."

Then, like now, he was mad at her for scaring him.

His thoughts gnawed at him as his whittled-thin stick snapped in two and the sun dipped into sinews of clouds strung along the horizon. He might as well head back. Pa wouldn't be happy about his backed-up chores.

Moments later he came close to stepping on a black snake making its way off a cooling boulder. Marcus was startled more by his inattention than by the snake.

Amos arrived at church on time, astride a horse Maylene hadn't seen before. The horse was a handsome bay gelding, looking cleaner and better fed than Amos's previous, sway-backed mount. Amos looked uncomfortable straddling a sidesaddle, and Maylene couldn't help smiling when she saw him wince as he dismounted.

After church, Maylene noticed her father fussing with Spit's harness. He kept looking over at Amos, who helped Maylene onto the saddle but appeared in no hurry to depart. Amos was rambling about the sermon, Maylene scarcely listening. Having never ridden a sidesaddle, Maylene wondered if she'd keep her balance. At length, Papa gave Amos a glare and climbed to his seat, slapping the check lines with unusual vigor. At that moment Maylene realized her father wanted to follow Amos and her home, not lead the way.

As soon as the Farley family was out of sight, Amos said, "Step out of that stirrup, I'm coming aboard."

He swung onto the horse, behind the saddle, and reached around Maylene for the reins. He gave the gelding an energetic kick. "Get up, Mack."

The horse flipped back his ears and tossed his head as he stepped out. Maylene didn't blame him.

Amos kept the reins taut, crowding her. He seemed oblivious.

Maylene tolerated the pressure of Amos's chest against her shoulder blades for a full minute before saying, "Slide back, you're mashing me."

Amos laughed and moved no more than a half inch. At the next sliding opportunity, when the horse took a slight misstep, he was right back. Maylene took interest in the passing upslope of tree-clad mountain.

Must this horse walk so slowly?

Amos was uncharacteristically quiet, his fingers fidgeting with the reins. Then, with a burst of relief, he found a topic.

In a too-loud voice he said, "How old are you?"

"I'm sixteen. And a half."

"Sixteen and a half. Have you ever been kissed?"

Maylene was taken aback. "Amos!"

"Aw, I'm just kiddin'. I just figure there are plenty of boys who'd like to try."

Maylene dashed for safer ground. "How old are you?"

"Nineteen. Without the half." He grinned.

"What about your family?"

"I'm the oldest. I've got two younger sisters and a younger brother. Caroline, Lura, and Caleb. There were others who died young. My Paw Paw and Maw Maw live with us, too, but Paw Paw is getting so he can't hardly walk no more."

"Up on Broomstraw?"

"Yeah."

"How do you know where I live?"

"I asked around." Amos used a shoulder to give her a little shove.

Amos pulled up Mack, dismounted just before the cabin came into view, and walked the remainder of the way up the farm lane. Maylene wasn't sure if she was annoyed or amused.

At dinner Margaret was too giggly, Melva too silent. Mama asked too many questions, and Papa was only a whisker the civil side of hostile. Maylene thought she would choke on the fried chicken, sweet potatoes, and pickled corn she normally would have consumed with a teen's ravenous enthusiasm. Mama had made everything so nice, she had to try.

Amos proved comfortable bragging about himself, in particular the work he was doing to fix up his grandpa's old cabin. He'd put a new roof on it, he said, and would have the inside all spruced up by spring. By all appearances, he enjoyed being the center of Mrs. Farley's attention. He said Yes, ma'am and No, sir, and he sat up straight as a pine trunk. He praised the food as fit for Christmas. He leapt up to pull out Sara Mae's chair, then Maylene's, when dishes were cleared.

Papa walked Amos to the door.

What Maylene didn't know was that Amos had the reputation of being something of a card-playing, snake-oil-selling sort who couldn't be trusted. Sara Mae reminded her husband that they oughtn't to cotton to rumors, but it was devilishly hard not to, especially when the subject of those rumors was courting their daughter. They waited for a flaw to reveal itself, like the rot in a potato that comes to light upon slicing.

Amos was in her thoughts constantly. Although he carried a scent of danger, Maylene was drawn like a mink to spawning fish. In comparison, Marcus was boyish. He had never called her "pretty," never pressed his chest against her back. He had never made her blush or quickened her pulse. He was child's play next to Amos.

Maylene wrote to her grandma, asking if she might have fabric for a dress she would make, a dress she and Melva could share.

The next Sunday, neither Marcus nor Amos came to church. Maylene found it necessary to check the back of her collar for an invisible flaw, to scrutinize the bench-back for an uncomfortable unevenness that had never existed before, and to glance backward when turning to whisper to Margaret. Each time, her stomach clenched with alarm. Where was he?

Her anxiety was relieved when Amos, riding the underfed roan of his first trips to church, showed up at the farm after dinner. Maylene wondered momentarily what had become of Mack, but she was immediately distracted by the bouquet of goldenrod and aster Amos presented.

"For my lady," he said with an extravagant bow.

"How pretty! I thank you kindly." Maylene would have given a little curtsey if not for fear of her sisters' ridicule. Must they be ever-present?

Flustered about what to do with the gift, Maylene glanced about. She stuffed the flowers into an empty milk pail and sent Margaret to the well for water.

It was October and the afternoon was mild. Amos suggested a walk.

"Let's go down to the river," Maylene said. "It's not far, maybe a mile. Margaret or Melva will have to come, of course."

"Of course." Amos managed a smile.

Maylene did her best to entertain Amos with fishing stories, but she sensed the same distractedness Amos had expressed the week before. Clearly, he had little interest in fish. She was grateful when extroverted Margaret took over, talking about her school classmates, sharing every rumor she could think of, and finally, to Maylene's surprise, asking Amos if he thought there would be war.

"Only if the Northerners want it," Amos answered. "We'll be pushed so far and no farther—then they'll have a thrashing comin'."

Margaret giggled the way she did when she was wound up. Her blond curls accentuated her merriment, bouncing with every turn of her head.

"Do you want to fight them?"

"No, ma'am! I want to settle down with a pretty girl and raise up a whole litter of young'uns." He gave Maylene a quick look.

Did he wink? Maylene felt the loathsome heat rising up her neck.

Margaret laughed without reserve.

The following Sunday the wind blew out of the northwest. Gray clouds swept across the sky with the urgency of migration, and leaves fell by the thousands, collecting in Madam's Creek and every hoof print and wagon rut. Maylene wore a shawl over her blue dress, heavy black stockings, and an extra petticoat. Only half the Lilly children warmed their bench, and Maylene knew why. Three atop Pal and two astride the mule left six on foot, and they took turns riding. The distance of nearly three miles necessitated shoes on all feet in the cold. Because the family didn't have eleven pairs of shoes at any given time, there were members who stayed home on chilly Sundays. Marcus was among those missing this day. In another month, the entire Lilly bench would sit vacant, and remain so until spring. It was a difficult journey down Madam's Creek in winter, with or without shoes.

Maylene had seen Amos arrive on the side-saddled bay as she hurried for the shelter of the small chapel. Amos evidently assumed one yes was good for all Sundays—he could escort Maylene home from church with impunity.

An hour later, as Maylene stepped out the door, a gallant arm appeared for her to take. She felt like a princess guided to her waiting steed and couldn't resist smiling up at Amos, who patted her hand.

Papa had given up the contest. He paid no attention to the couple but put the mules smartly in motion as soon as Mama and the girls were settled. Within minutes, however, Amos and Maylene overtook the Farley entourage. Papa stood, bent over, next to Dolly, inspecting a hoof.

"Need some help?" Amos called out as he pulled Mack to a stop.

"Naw, she just picked up a stone. It's out." Papa patted Dolly without looking at Amos.

Lacking an excuse to remain, Amos gave the horse a kick. "Get up, Max."

Max? Maylene felt colder. It's not his horse. Or saddle either.

Now, impatient for speed, Amos wanted to put distance between them and Maylene's trailing family. He kicked again, and Mack, or Max, responded with a trot. The road was rough even at a walk—a spine-jarring calamity at a trot. Maylene snatched up the dancing mane with both fists.

Amos laughed and said, "Don't worry, I won't let you fall." An arm went around her waist.

Aware of inattention, the bay returned to a walk.

"Get up!" Amos barked. He released Maylene long enough to slap the gelding's flank. A brisk trot ensued. The arm was back around Maylene, pulling her close. Amos laughed again, Maylene did not.

The horse had enough sense to know foolishness and tried again to slow his pace. Amos kicked and shouted, repeating this urging again and again as the horse labored up the creek toward the Farley farm.

Maylene knew it was uncomfortable for the horse to carry so much extra weight behind the saddle. She'd had enough. "Let him walk."

"What, and spoil our fun?" Amos gave another thump with his heels.

Maylene saw sweat beginning to darken the horse's flanks.

Amos didn't slow the charge to a walk until negotiating the turn onto the farm and across the bridge that spanned the creek. To Maylene's surprise, he pulled to a stop fifty yards shy of the cabin.

Maylene was trying to solve the puzzle of dismounting from the odd saddle with a man in her way when she took in Amos's cheeks alight with cold or excitement, she didn't know which.

"Now tell me that wasn't a jolly ride! Your ma and pa must be a half-mile behind. I've finally got you all to myself."

With that he grabbed her shoulders and put his mouth on hers so fast she didn't have a chance to protest. She couldn't move away without risk of falling.

It was her first kiss, but nothing like she had imagined. It was hard and hungry, almost mean. She braced one hand on her elevated knee and used the other to push against Amos's chest, hard, forcing Amos off balance enough to release her and clutch the saddle to avoid pulling them both to the ground.

"What are you doing?" She hated the tremor in her voice. "We can't!"

"I knew it! You've never been kissed, have you?"

"That's my business, not yours." Her jaw trembled. She held back tears. Why was she close to crying?

Maylene searched the weedy road behind them, longing to see the waggling ears of Spit and Dolly appear as they made the bend and slight climb from the creek. She kicked her left foot out of the stirrup, unhitched her right leg from the pommel, leapt to the ground before Amos could stop her, and began striding toward the cabin. Amos ran after her, snatching her arm.

"What are you mad about?" he demanded, spinning her to face him. "It was only a kiss."

She hated the pressure of his fingers on her arm. She hated the anger in his voice.

"You took me off guard. It was rude. It was...." She wanted to say "ungentlemanly" but she was starting to lose control.

Stop it, stop it! Her self-instruction, meant to be commanding, was a plea devoid of authority.

"Well, before you get all high and almighty with me, missy, I don't see a line of suitors at your door. You might well give an inch to the one you've got!"

Maylene found herself speechless with rage. She pulled away, but Amos tightened his grip on her arm. She feared she was too close to the kind of crying and shouting fight she thought she'd outgrown to trust herself with more than a look of fury she hoped spoke for her. But it made her feel weak-minded not to have a ready response, and that fueled the fire to brighter blaze.

"You… must…," she was going to say "leave at once," but stopped as her voice cracked and she heard hoofbeats.

Impossible. Amos dropped her arm. There came the mules. Always more lively in the homeward direction, they must have responded readily to Papa's demand for speed.

Maylene was still breathing hard when Papa reined in the team.

"Funny place to pull up." Bob Farley eyed Amos without humor. He didn't need to slice the potato to smell the rot.

CHAPTER FOUR

Maylene had never felt like a fool before, a bona fide, first-class fool. Her tears were more about that than anything that night, when she lay crying next to Melva in their shared bed.

Melva whispered over her sister's shoulder, "What happened?"

"Nothing. It was just a quarrel."

"Can you fix it?"

"No."

"Are you sure? You like Amos, don't you?"

"I don't know anymore."

That was a lie. Maylene did know. She did not like Amos Wallace. She lay awake reviewing all the things about him she did not like. She didn't like the way he treated the horse that wasn't his. She didn't like his slick confidence, which had gone in an eye-blink from appealing to revolting. She cringed at the memory of his chest pressed against her, his arm around her, as if she belonged to him. And more than anything else, she hated the memory of his kiss. Hard, stale, rough, demanding.

Dear Papa. Somehow he had known.

Well before dawn, Maylene slipped out of bed and crept down the winding loft steps. She used the poker to stir embers in the fireplace and coaxed a few sticks of kindling into flames. Now she would have to stay up to tend the fire, but she might as well—sleep would not come. She pulled a quilt off the back of her mother's rocker and sat down, drawing the blanket around her shoulders. Looking into the flames, Maylene tried to sort out her brief attraction to Amos. Older, taller, more confident, more experienced…. Had she looked to him to launch her into adulthood, prove something to herself? Was it his good looks that flattered her, made her feel proud to be seen with him? Maybe it was the way his eyes followed her every move, making her feel exciting and pretty. Yet she had sensed he half-listened to her words. Had he shown any genuine interest in getting to know her? Maylene couldn't deny an uneasy suspicion she had willfully overlooked every warning sign that Amos was reckless, arrogant, and focused on his own gains—the kind of man capable of making her life miserable.

Her thoughts turned to Marcus, who had scarcely crossed her mind in weeks. Marcus who would never mistreat a horse, Marcus who would never boast, never do or say anything to make her uncomfortable. Marcus who knew her better than her own sisters did. Marcus who would never have her first kiss.

"Simpleton!"

Amos, to his credit, did come cautiously back to church the next week, arriving late. The Farleys were ready for him. They formed a phalanx around Maylene and made such a hasty exit there could be no mistaking their message. Maylene, head down, took a pointed interest in her feet.

Amos never came back.

The Lillys, however, were absent and missed the snub. Maylene feared the family wouldn't return to church until spring, and she wouldn't see Marcus until then. She rode home in a brooding silence that saddened her sisters. Even the mules carried their heads lower than usual on the climb back up the creek.

Sara Mae had anticipated this possibility, however, and had given her husband instructions the week before. Bob and Sara Mae were a half-mile ahead of Amos Wallace all along.

Bob Farley liked his son-in-law, Corbin Radcliff. Broad of shoulder, snub-nosed, green-eyed, and dark haired, Corbin was an able man of even temperament, a good and decent man, the kind of man who would take readily to fatherhood and stand by his wife. But Bob had a special fondness for Marcus, who was quick of mind and made him think, at times, of what Robin would be like. Robin would be eleven by now. Bob knew, he kept track.

The bond between Bob and Marcus grew by virtue of bees. Bob had a number of hives at the wooded edge of one pasture, well above the floodplain. He had taught his daughters to use smoke to remove combs from the hives, but there came a day things went badly. The bees were in a foul mood for reasons unclear, and a breeze kicked up at just the wrong moment, dispersing the smoke. The bees had Mary and Melva and him to choose from, and it was Melva they went after. Her eyes swelled shut and she was feverish for days. It scared him.

Marcus happened to be there the next time he went into the hives. The boy was calm and steady as a turtle in the sun. Not a bit afraid. It eased Bob to have his daughters uninvolved, and the extraction went like clockwork. From then on, he preferred to work with Marcus, always sending him home with a generous supply of honey.

But Marcus hadn't been around this fall, and Bob had done the work alone. He had left an ample amount of honey untapped, however—more than the bees needed to get through the winter, he felt sure. It wouldn't hurt to go back in.

Bob had spoken with Quentin the Sunday of the wagon sprint, asking him to send Marcus down the following Sunday. He was a little uneasy about his choice of the Sabbath but didn't want to pull Marcus away from his work-day duties, and honey extraction wasn't really work, if you went about it right. Neither he nor Sara Mae considered refusal, no matter how

Marcus might feel about facing Amos. The boy would not let them down.

Marcus made sure to leave home late enough to miss Sunday dinner at the Farley's. He saddled the gray workhorse, Pal, with wooden motions, as if he were unfamiliar with tack. He mounted with the stiffness of an aged man and groped for the right stirrup.

Maylene and Amos. He could hear Junior's sing-song chant in his head.

For the first time in her life, Maylene was on edge about seeing Marcus. What must he think of her, accepting the attentions of a man so beneath him? Would he talk to her? Shun her? The thought of Marcus turning a cold shoulder was unbearable.

The afternoon was warm enough that Maylene needed no excuse to be outside. She sat on the porch mending a harness strap as Marcus approached the steps.

"Afternoon, Marcus." She tried to sound like it was any afternoon.

"Maylene." He looked up at her, then quickly away, scanning. "Your pa around?"

"He's already at the hives."

"Good." Marcus hurried away.

As soon as he was out of sight, Maylene threw the harness strap onto the porch floor and stood. She couldn't sit still another second. She needed to walk.

Maylene circled the pastures and climbed high into the woods. She found a fallen buckeye to sit on, where she could watch Marcus and her father, unseen. In a cloud of smoke, they worked almost in slow-motion, every step measured, every arm movement gracefully precise. Even from her distant perch, she could tell they talked little, but communicated more with subtle gestures as they cut comb from three hives and placed it gently in a wooden bucket. Bees swirled about them but few landed. The boy and man made no effort to whisk them away.

Stay, Maylene begged, fearful Marcus would leave as soon as the task was completed.

She might have known her pa would find a way to detain him, lingering over the division of honey as Maylene made her way back down the wooded slope. Marcus saw her emerge from the woods. Bob looked up from his sticky work.

"She's been wanting to talk to you," Bob said. "I can finish up here."

Marcus hesitated, feeling his palms turn clammy. Wanting to talk to you... How was he going to handle it if she told him she was planning to marry Amos Wallace? Surely not so soon. But Amos had a reputation as a lady's man....

"Yes, sir." Marcus headed in Maylene's direction. With every step, he told himself to be a man.

Maylene spoke first.

"I've been wanting to see you, to have a word. I was afraid you'd run off." The words were spilling out in a chaotic stampede. She didn't know what was coming next.

"I don't know your feelings. Your intentions. What I mean is, I would be pleased, it would give me pleasure.... I'd be right honored if you'd keep your hat in the ring."

Marcus stared with his mouth open. He reminded Maylene of a baby robin.

A few steps to his right was a bald spot, where Spit and Dolly liked to roll. Marcus walked to it. Not knowing what else to do, Maylene followed.

Marcus used the toe of his boot to draw a square in the dry soil. Then he took off his sun-faded black hat and dropped it directly in the center. It landed with a soft pluff and a cloud of dust.

Maylene clamped her hand over her mouth, overcome with a fit of hysterics. It was all she could do to keep from laughing aloud, and tears of mirth stung her eyes.

Marcus let out a great exhaled breath and smiled at Maylene with such unadulterated happiness, Maylene knew she'd go from laughing to crying if he didn't say something at once.

He managed just two words, "No Amos?"

"No Amos."

With that Marcus snatched his hat from the ground with the grace of a barn swallow, returned the powdered garment to his head, and headed for the barn and his waiting booty of honey.

Maylene returned to the cabin. As she climbed the steps, Marcus's head and shoulders appeared out of the open barn door. "It's time for persimmons. I'll be down for you next Sunday if you like."

"I'll be waiting on you."

Maylene went inside to help her mother knead bread. A little later she remembered her discarded project on the porch and went out to gather harness, awl, and strips of rawhide. The sun had long since dropped below the wooded ridge rising high above the creek's west side, committing the farm to the long twilight of mountain hollows. Her father approached from the barn. Marcus must be gone.

Then she heard, coming down the creek with water and darkness, a distant yet unmistakable sound: a drawn-out, lung-emptying whoop. Someone sounded happy.

CHAPTER FIVE

There was nothing but talk of secession that winter, after Lincoln's election. South Carolina was first, a few days before Christmas. Mississippi followed suit. In rapid succession, Florida, Alabama, Georgia, Louisiana, and Texas pulled out of the Union. Virginia teetered on the rim of the abyss.

Junior Lilly's mind was made up early—he supported the Union. He and Quentin had words.

Quentin said, "We are Virginians first, son. For four generations we've been Virginians. We'll not be ruled by the North."

Junior was adamant. "It's the Union above all else, Pa. How can we allow the country to break into pieces? It's the hot-headed plantation masters who started this. I'll not fight for their right to fan themselves in the shade."

"You'll bring shame on this family."

"Is that all you care about, what others say?"

"I care about loyalty."

"So do I!"

Soon there was palpable tension in the Lilly home, father versus son. Suzanne's strategy was to interest Junior in taking a wife. Hopeful that romance would help him forget his new-found idealistic zeal, she considered potential mates but found the list of options unpromising. Melva Farley, nearly a year older than Junior, had never shown the faintest interest in him. Junior's former classmate, Beth Ellen Jones, had such a severe acne affliction that she was deemed hopelessly unsightly. Verna Parker was simply too... simple. And Kate Ellison—the one girl Junior had briefly courted—had recently run off with a circuit-riding Methodist.

Marcus and Johnny listened to both sides of the argument but stayed out of the quarrel, intuiting the wisdom of silence. Their sisters—Eliza, Rachel, Vesta, and Louella—asked questions and were told war was unlikely, certainly not here in the mountains. Pay no mind. The little boys, Calvin and Lester, were too young to pause in their play.

Bob and Sara Mae Farley began to feel a special gratitude for having daughters.

The first week of February, representatives of the seven seceded states met in Montgomery, Alabama, to form the Confederate States of America. That same day, Bob Farley picked up a package from Charlottesville addressed to his third daughter. It was a bundle of fabric.

Maylene began a dress intended as a gift for Margaret, who was growing like a bean sprout. Maylene had never before asked her grandma for anything, and found the reminder of Amos vaguely bitter, like the taste of mustard greens.

Nine days after the package's arrival, on Maylene's seventeenth birthday, a state convention was called to order to determine if Virginia would secede.

Several weeks later, the matter remained unsettled. The day was breezy and unseasonably mild. It was the ninth of March, and Maylene remembered. She climbed to Robin's sandstone marker after breakfast, and there she sat, looking out at the valley below. From this spot she could see a bend of the New as it made its way north to its deep gorge. Farther north it joined the Kanawha, which joined the Ohio. She would like to see those rivers, too, with Marcus. There was talk of a new rail line coming, which would follow the New all the way to Kanawha and Ohio. Given the landscape, it was hard to imagine such a feat. New River had spatulate floodplains here and there, like clamshells threaded onto a tortuously convoluted rope, but for the most part its banks merged either with sheer cliffs or with slopes so steep they were daunting even for deer.

A grayish-green bird with a pale breast landed on a redbud branch nearby, interrupting Maylene's thoughts. It pumped its tail as it eyed Maylene, and a smile spread across the girl's face. A phoebe! Marcus would want to know—a phoebe in March was noteworthy as one of the first signs of spring. Maylene would tell him as soon as he came back to church. Papa had already started organizing a crew to work on the road, ravaged by winter ice and spring runoff.

Marcus had been nearly absent that winter, making only a few trips down the holler to the Farley farm. Maylene had no way of knowing he had devoted every weather-worthy Sunday to breaking the Sabbath. He had cleared an oval of brush and begun felling trees and shaping logs for what he would build there.

Marcus turned seventeen in April of 1861, the month the war began. Virginia's delegation voted not to secede that same month, but voted again after Arkansas, Tennessee, and North Carolina joined the Confederacy. By the time the corn reached the bottom of Maylene's skirts that summer, Virginia had seceded from the Union and there was no turning back.

Newspapers were purchased as quickly as they arrived in Jumping Branch, and news of the war spread at the speed the most athletic horses could master routes from store to mill or ferry, and from there to church. Once word reached churches, it was known by all but the most reclusive shut-ins.

Maylene was filled with apprehension. When they were out of earshot of Johnny, Melva, and Margaret, she asked Marcus, "Will you go?"

"Only if I'm conscripted. I don't see it as our fight."

"As a Confederate?"

"I can't see siding against Virginia, even if she's wrong."

"What about Junior?"

"He'll be gone any day. Ma and Pa can't talk him out of it. He's going up to Washington to enlist."

"How will he get there?"

"There are some others going. He says someone has an extra mule. They're going all the way to Harpers Ferry and picking up a train to Washington. I don't know where he got the money or provisions. He's not saying."

"Is it dangerous? Could they be arrested?"

"I don't think so. Not yet."

"I don't want you to go."

"Don't worry about it, Maylene. I'm not planning on going anywhere." Marcus lifted another rock in search of a hellgrammite. They'd run out of fishing bait.

Marcus felt differently about Maylene after the Amos incident. She had become a woman in his eyes, a woman other men noticed and coveted. He couldn't risk taking her for granted anymore. He got urges when he was around her, and he didn't know what to do with them. He knew the basics, at least he thought he did, from reading the Bible and being around livestock. But sex was still murky, shrouded in secrecy. Did people really do it in the manner of animals? And why would a woman allow a man to do that to her? Once she had all the babies she wanted, wouldn't she put a stop to it? It was impossible to imagine Maylene wanting him that way.

He was skittish in his wariness of offending her and wondered what Amos had done so irrevocably wrong. But that was her business. He wasn't going to ask.

Maylene, for her part, was beginning to want another shot at kissing. It would have to be better with Marcus, and it seemed time for them to move past the sibling roles they'd played so long. Was she not pretty to Marcus? She wondered how he saw her.

Their chance came unexpectedly. They were sitting on stumps that served as chairs, stringing green beans in the shade of the barn, when Margaret abandoned them. Papa was hoeing the garden, out of sight on the other side of the barn. Mama was at that time of month when she didn't feel well and had gone inside to lie down. Having seized the opportunity, Melva had vanished, most likely with their latest novel.

Margaret stood up, throwing her last processed beans into the large wooden bowl at the trio's feet. "I'm sick to death of these beans. I'm going down to the creek to cool off."

"All right. Suit yourself," Maylene said without looking up.

Margaret strode away, leaving Maylene shaking her head over the beans pooled in her skirt. "Lord, but she can be a willful child."

Marcus finished the collection in his shirttail before turning to Maylene. "It's nice to be alone for a spell."

Maylene gave him a quick smile and returned her focus to the present bean, expertly removing the string and snapping the bean in two. She dropped the halves into the bowl.

Marcus didn't reach into the garden basket for another handful, Maylene noticed.

"I've been working on something since last fall...." He stopped.

Maylene gave him her full attention.

"What?"

"I'm building a cabin."

It was Maylene's turn to gape. "You're building a cabin and didn't tell me? By yourself?"

"Mostly by myself. Johnny helps me some. I wanted it to be a surprise."

Maylene didn't dare hope, but of course she did. She felt her heart's tempo quicken. "Can I see it sometime? How far along is it?"

"The chimney and outer walls are done. I'm near done with the roof, but I need to cut another cedar for shingles. There's inside work to do yet, and the windows. And I want to make a porch."

"Where is it?"

"I'll show you."

Maylene fell silent, groping for another question. Marcus spun on his stump-top, to face her directly.

"I'm going to live in that cabin when it's done. I haven't had as much time as I hoped for, but I reckon it will be ready next spring."

"You must be proud."

"I will be." Marcus leaned forward. "Please don't move."

Maylene froze and closed her eyes. There was a sensation on her lips, almost imagined, as if a swallowtail had landed for an instant and taken flight again. She opened her eyes.

Marcus was grinning at her.

"Did you just kiss me?"

"I think I did, just barely."

Maylene wasn't satisfied with that butterfly landing. "Will you do that again?"

This time the touch was more like the soft nuzzle of a horse. Brief but firm. Maylene felt Marcus's breath, warm and welcome on her face. She opened her eyes again. The kiss had made whole new parts of her body come to life. She stood up, baffled, smiling, thrilled.

Marcus was already on his feet, his face crimson. He was having his own reaction and felt he would rather die than have Maylene notice. He needn't have worried—her eyes were fixed on his glowing face.

"I've never seen you blush before."

"It won't be the last time if you let me kiss you again."

His urge to take her in his arms was fierce, but she might feel the structure that had materialized in his pants. When Maylene took a step toward him, he took a step back, bumping into the stump and nearly falling.

"Don't tempt me, Maylene," he said, sounding strangely desperate to them both. "You're much too pretty!"

He said it.

Recovering his balance and a degree of composure, Marcus said, "I'll go ask your pa if I can bring you up on Sunday. I'll show you the cabin."

"He's in the garden."

"I know."

Maylene was enchanted. The cabin sat on a natural bench overlooking the Lilly hay and corn fields. There was a steep wooded slope behind it, pastures adjacent and above, to the east. Marcus explained that he had positioned the building to face south. It would receive ample winter sun. The woods would shade it on summer afternoons. The chimney was a work of art. Marcus had scoured the mountainside for each stone, so carefully fit together as to require no mortar. Hand-hewn chestnut beams crossed the ceiling. Squared logs chinked with split sticks and mortared with clay made up the thick walls. Fresh, fragrant oak boards covered the floor. A ladder was already in place to access the loft, which awaited flooring. Cedar shingles on the roof neared completion.

"It's a masterpiece," Maylene said.

"Not that, but it will do. The last thing will be the porch. But there will still be one thing missing."

"What's that?" Maylene was thinking steps would be missing. She didn't see what was coming until she looked at Marcus. His face had gone colorless, and he looked on the verge of vomiting.

Then, she knew, and she could think of no way to help him.

Marcus squeezed the words out of a rigid throat. "It will need you."

Maylene felt the need to sit down, but there was nothing to sit on, save the floor.

"Are you saying…." She stopped. He would have to ask her.

Marcus unfroze himself and stepped forward in the dim light of the cabin's interior. He took both Maylene's hands. "I'm trying. I'm trying to say I want you to be here with me. My Maylene. My… wife. Would you consent to marry me when I finish the cabin next year? I know we could move in with Ma and Pa, but I want us to have our own home. Just us. Here."

Maylene felt tears burgeoning up from wherever they wait in hiding. Marcus stroked the backs of her hands with his thumbs, waiting. He no longer looked scared. He looked happy, like someone who had gotten wonderful, long-awaited news. Yet serenely so, as if he'd seen it coming all along.

Having gotten the words out, Marcus was limp with relief. He sank into the luxurious knowledge he had carried in the marrow of his bones since he was a young boy, yet somehow failed to trust in recent months—Maylene Farley had always loved him.

Maylene nodded, gave up on words, and hurled herself into his arms.

He held her tightly, saying, "I can't fault you for crying. The prospect of a whole lifetime with me would bring anyone to tears."

His flippant words didn't prevent desire from engulfing him. It was so powerful he didn't dare prolong the embrace but led Maylene back into the sunlight of the day, a new day, a day completely unlike the one they'd left when they stepped inside.

The Lillys were delighted but not surprised by the news. There had been no question what Marcus had in mind when he began spending every spare minute on his pet project. Junior would have ribbed him mercilessly, and Marcus felt a pang. He'd never gotten an ounce of pleasure from his older brother's heavy-handed teasing, but he would have welcomed it now. Junior had left two days earlier with a small, secretive group of Union recruits.

It was on the way home, riding the Lilly mule next to Marcus on Pal, that Maylene thought of her father. "What about Papa? Weren't you supposed to ask him first?"

"We had a little talk in the garden last week."

"You did? What did he say?"

"He said he'd been hoping someone would take you off his hands."

Maylene gave him a look. Marcus guffawed.

"Naw. He said the decision was yours, but he'd be mighty pleased to have me join the family."

"It's like you already are a member of the family."

"You think so?"

Maylene's face clouded. "You can't go off to war."

"Not planning to, Maylene. That's about the last thing I want right now."

The war, however, was on the move, and it cared little for the wishes or dreams in its path. The battles of Bull Run and Manassas raged in Virginia that summer. The battles of Ball's Bluff and Belmont that fall in Virginia and Missouri. The Confederates suffered staggering losses at Fort Donelson in Tennessee the following winter.

As the conflict grew in scale and casualties, the demand for soldiers escalated.

In April of 1862, Marcus Lilly turned eighteen. He and Maylene had been together every Sunday since their engagement the previous summer, with the exception of two when the snow was too deep even for Pal. They sat together at church, held hands when they thought no one was looking, and managed rare kisses and rarer caresses. They used any excuse to touch and became accustomed to the heady rush of arousal that always accompanied their times together. They flirted. They laughed. They made those around them smile with mixtures of memory and the benign sort of envy lovers evoke.

Marcus was torn between wanting to spend time with Maylene and his urgent desire to complete the cabin. With Junior gone, there was more work for him and Johnny—his time was more squeezed than ever. He would make a fire in the new fireplace, hang a fat-burning lamp, and work long after dark, long after his fingers and toes had gone numb. But the work went slowly, with every board shaped by hand—flooring for the loft, shelves, a dry sink, framing for windows and door... By April, his goal was June. There was furniture yet to build, including a bed.

It was a goal thwarted. In April of 1862, the Confederate States of America instituted a draft. With a short list of exceptions, all men between the ages of 18 and 35 must serve for three years.

Although Marcus had anticipated conscription, the news came as a shock. He'd thought he had more time. Maylene was aghast and begged him to run away with her. They would go west, go to Canada, go somewhere, anywhere, away from the dreadful war.

"You realize I'd likely be jailed or shot if I were caught?"

Maylene had no answer. She was simply terrified, grasping at impossibilities.

Marcus had been somewhat more of a realist. At times, alone and pounding pegs into place, he heard the echo of his blows rebounding from the surrounding slopes. Or was it the drums of war? A shiver would scamper down his spine like a squirrel down an oak trunk.

But, like everything else they read about in the papers, the war felt far away. Marcus and Maylene held onto hope of a brief conflict, quickly resolved. And although they had sometimes felt guilty for being blissful when others were suffering and dying, they had maintained belief in the safety of their isolated world these past nine months as the cabin and their plans took shape. Now, with the stroke of a distant pen, that sense of refuge had been annihilated, plunging them into a hard-edged world of frightful strife.

It didn't make sense to either of them to marry when they were miserable, and hadn't a bed. Everything was rushed. Confused. Teary. Adding to their sense of turmoil came news of Union soldiers sweeping across Mercer County, adjacent to Raleigh County to the south. As Confederate troops retreated from the town of Princeton, they set it afire to keep stockpiles of supplies from falling into enemy hands. Nearly the entire town, including the courthouse, was destroyed.

Marcus and Maylene could feel the dragon's breath on the back of their necks. They would wait for the monster to die. Marcus would go, and Maylene would stay and pray he would come back to her. They'd marry when the cabin was ready and they were happy again. They told each other that image would see them through.

But three years. Who would they be by then?

Marcus would have preferred to slip away without a good-bye. But he had to ride right past the Farley farm on his way down Madam's Creek and onward, down New River to the crossing at New Richmond. Geography was not in his favor, nor the fact that Maylene would never forgive him.

Maylene had told herself a dozen times she wouldn't cry. She'd already broken down more than once in Marcus's presence, and she knew it rattled him. He would hold her and stroke her hair, making shushing sounds, but he could find no words to take the pain away.

It was dawn, a spring day. An oriole and a cardinal forced solos above a riotous background of songbird chorus. Every grass blade was bejeweled with dew. Mist rose from the creek. Dogwoods were beginning to blossom along the edges of the woods, in shouts of white. Under normal circumstances, it would have been beautiful, the kind of day that erases winter's hardships with its fragrant, blooming, buzzing optimism.

Marcus dismounted and walked up to the cabin as sunlight broke into the hollow.

The Farleys were assembled on the porch. Bob and Sara Mae stood as a study in contrasts. The one nearly a head taller was lanky and square-jawed, with a prominent chin, strong nose, and overgrown, sun-bleached eyebrows. The pert-nosed other, without quite being plump, exhibited roundness in her every feature—eyes, face, bosom, tummy, and derriere—as if constructed entirely of spherical shapes. The one reversal in curves was found in their hair, with Bob being the one adorned with curls. Their one shared feature was the autumn-sky blue of their eyes.

But along with every other aspect of the morning, the Farleys blurred to near-incomprehension as Marcus reached the top of the steps. Clearly in no mood for speeches, Maylene's mismatched parents offered hugs. Melva and Margaret followed suit and trailed their parents back inside to a flavorless breakfast, leaving Maylene for the final send-off.

"I'll be on my way, then," said Marcus.

"Take this." Maylene handed him a small cloth package, wrapped with twine. "It's johnnycakes and boiled eggs."

Marcus tucked the bundle into a leather satchel slung across his chest. "Thank you."

They held each other hard but without tarrying. "Come home to me," Maylene whispered in his ear.

"I shall. In two shakes of a lamb's tail," and Marcus was down the steps.

He remounted his newly acquired horse, twisted for a last look, and forced a faint smile before reining toward the creek and a future he faced with dry-mouth dread.

CHAPTER SIX

I t was less than three weeks after Marcus's departure when Maylene was approached by a member of the Baptist congregation. It was Mrs. Nivens who buttonholed her after church, and Maylene cringed inwardly, knowing there was rarely a pleasant outcome from such an encounter.

Mrs. Nivens was a diminutive widow in her early sixties. She had small eyes and a pinched face, overall, a withered look. She had found her husband dead next to her in bed on a morning twenty or more years ago. Childless, Mrs. Nivens had lived alone ever since, surviving on her dogged toughness and scant need of nourishment. She was known to all as pious and devout, yet tragically lacking in kindness. It was fortunate her husband, Jack, had never heard the wisecracks about the shriveling effect on his manhood proximity to Polly Nivens likely had. The absence of children made perfect sense when one stopped and thought about it.

Maylene recalled her mother saying, "Jack Nivens probably died on purpose to put an end to the mistake of marrying that vile woman."

Mrs. Nivens, rushing up to Maylene that Sunday, wasted no time on formalities. "Oh, you poor child, you must be worried sick!"

"Why?"

The gossip widened her puny eyes in mock surprise. "Then you haven't heard? There's been a terrible conflict at Lewisburg. Hundreds killed. Our poor Rebel boys lost the fight and had to flee across the Greenbrier. They burned the bridge to save themselves."

"No, I didn't know."

"Oh, it was dreadful, I tell you. Fighting right there in town. Blood running in the streets! I'm praying for our Marcus, and I know you'll do the same."

Maylene stood stunned, with panic and anger vying for the upper hand.

Be quiet, you horrid little witch! She wanted to grab Mrs. Nivens' bony shoulders and shake her until her wicked tongue was still. But it was too late. That tongue had done its damage, and relished the privilege.

Maylene croaked, "Cavalry?"

"That I don't know. I would think it likely. And I learned there's a whole regiment of Yankees camped on Flat Top Mountain. On Flat Top! Next thing you know they'll be on White Oak and making raids right here on Madam's Creek. Lord help us if they do!"

Bob Farley had heard enough to intervene. "It's good of you to express your concerns, but there are many rumors afloat these days."

Good of you? Maylene's mounting fury turned on her father.

Mrs. Nivens pushed back her shoulders, aiming her chin like a weapon at the disapproving face above her. "It's no battle rumor, I can assure you, Mr. Farley. I heard it from Billy Dodd's wife, and he heard it at the Ferry from a Lewisburg resident who witnessed the entire fight! And Billy's cousin lives on the Flat Top side of White Oak, and he's seen the Union troops himself."

"Well, we'll get the details from the paper, then. Come along, Maylene. Your ma isn't feeling well."

Maylene noted one of her father's rare lies.

On the way home, Bob sought to comfort. "You know how that woman exaggerates. We can't become fretful over another of her tall tales. It was probably a skirmish. And I am entirely confident Marcus is still in training. He wouldn't be sent into a conflict so soon."

"You don't know that!" Maylene was seething, and her father, though she knew he was undeserving, was her only outlet.

"Maybe not with certainty, but there's another thing to consider. My understanding is that Lewisburg is not within the Rangers' territory. I don't believe they would have been there."

Maylene fumed at her father's willful naivety. "They could have been nearby. They could have been called on to assist."

"Don't borrow trouble, Maylene. We must assume the best until we know more."

Maylene, seated next to her father, was going to snap, That's easy enough for you to say! but found such a tightness in her throat the words didn't make their way out. She twisted the skirt of her dress in her hands, thinking, It's probably not even true.... But if it is true, he wasn't there. But even if he was there, he wasn't hurt. But if he was hurt, it was nothing serious, but if it was serious, he won't die, but....

She was working herself desperately close to worst-case scenario and didn't know how to stop the momentum of her runaway imagination. She turned to her mother, seated on her other side, with the frightened eyes of a nightmare-bedeviled child.

Sara Mae smiled back and pressed a hand over one of Maylene's fists. "Just consider the source, honey. Mrs. Nivens could make it snow in July. Don't let her prattle scare you."

Papa added, "And I talked to the men at Meador's. Those Union boys on Flat Top—they are sitting around with nothing to do, like every day's a Sunday, waiting to be told to go somewhere else. That somewhere else won't be Madam's Creek."

He noticed Spit was lollygagging. "Hup there, Spit! Don't make Dolly do all the work." He let a check line drop painlessly on Spitfire's rump to punctuate his complaint—and the mule responded with a snort and a faintly brisker pace— then completed his thought, "I fear Mrs. Nivens will be sorely disappointed."

Sara Mae did her best not to react, but her husband's quick glance ruined the effort, forcing a spasmodic giggle out of her. She turned it into a cough, for Maylene's sake, but didn't escape her daughter's wounded look that said, How can you make light of this?

At the earliest opportunity, by which time Maylene was badly on edge and unfocused from lack of sleep, Maylene and her pa rode the mules to Meador's Store to buy the Richmond paper, which was delivered only once a week. As Bob was making payment for the Sunday edition of *The Daily Dispatch*, Maylene tore the paper from under his arm. She spread it open and found an account of the battle under the heading, "The Campaign in Southwestern Virginia."

Bob was alarmed to see tears well in her eyes, but she said without looking up, "He wasn't there," closed the paper, handed it back, and walked out of the cluttered store.

Bob paused to read the short article and found his vision blurred, to his surprise, by tears of his own. He could just make out "the 22nd and 45th Virginia" and "Finney's Battalion." There was no mention of Marcus's company.

He felt a surge of relief for Maylene, and more. Losing Marcus, he realized, would be rather like losing Robin a second time. And his words of reassurance hadn't been any more convincing for him than they had been for Maylene.

Bob Farley drew a sleeve across his eyes and patted a vest pocket before following his daughter out to the mules. Maylene hadn't seen him place a small envelope there as she frantically pored over the paper. It held a letter from Marcus, postmarked one day before the Lewisburg conflict.

Maylene's relief was profound, and she prayed her thankfulness that Marcus remained, by all evidence, alive and well. But there remained the shock of having the war intrude in such a personal way. No longer was it restricted to accounts in newspapers of distant battles. For the first time, one could travel to as near a place as Pack's Ferry and hear a firsthand account of bloodshed in an adjacent county. Maylene had tried to believe Princeton's destruction was a fluke of proximity, but now Lewisburg....

Marcus was anything but safe.

Marcus, along with a number of others—including Maylene's brother-in-law, Corbin Radcliff—from Raleigh and nearby counties, was mustered in as a member of Thurmond's Partisan Rangers by virtue of the timely acquisition of a horse. The black gelding came to the Lillys as inheritance from an unmarried aunt of Quentin's. Marcus saw him as a sign the Lilly luck would hold. The Rangers served primarily as scouts and spies, with their field of duty in the mountains, where Marcus felt at home. It was hard living, to be sure, but without the infantry horrors of the battlefield.

Marcus became devoted to Blackjack, who proved to be a well-trained, able-minded, and amiable horse. He made some friends and discerned which men were rough and short-tempered, best sidestepped. The ease with which he procured turkeys and squirrels, gathered puffball mushrooms, snagged fish, and otherwise provided supplemental food for his hungry campmates enhanced his popularity, and he was soon honored with an Enfield rifle taken from a captured Federal soldier. The rifle was a superior weapon to the cavalry shotgun Marcus was happy to relinquish.

Corbin liked to say, "We've gotta keep Marcus alive, he's our commissary."

The usual fare of pickled beef and cornbread was sadly inadequate. All the men were hungry and became rail-thin, although Marcus and many others pretty much started out that way. A man didn't grow up on a mountain farm with a slew of siblings and carry extra meat on his bones.

There were good times making music, playing cards and practical jokes. Marcus took pleasure in seeing unfamiliar turf, the sense of discovery that came with each new village, farm, cascading stream, and highland meadow that punctuated the forested mountains of the Rangers' constant travels. But almost every other aspect of his new life sliced against the grain of who he was. His life was regimented, not his own. The Rangers' clandestine doings involved lies, thievery in the name of "military necessity," and deceit in many forms. The men collected reports of Union sympathizers as they conned and bullied people into giving up names and meeting places.

Marcus chafed. He wasn't the spying or coercing type. Easier for him were the hours in Blackjack's company scouting for Union troops and couriers, as well as long rides guarding Confederate supply routes. Even then, he was unable to escape the pitiful sight of men dragged from their homes and arrested for "treasonous acts"—such as voting against secession or feeding Yankees—or arrested on suspicion of desertion or spying while attempting to visit a wounded family member. Even delivering clothing to a poorly equipped soldier could result in arrest. It was not uncommon for a malicious charge to be made. Some found the war an expedient way to settle an old grudge and had a neighbor arrested as a Union man when he was nothing but an apolitical farmer trying to keep his family alive.

The same sorts of arrests occurred for the same sorts of reasons at the hands of Union forces. Families across the Virginia mountains learned to dread the approach of uniformed men of either persuasion.

As well, the Rangers knew danger—they sniped and were sniped upon. Marcus aimed high, grazing hats.

Because he took to heart the tenets of his religious upbringing, his faith only added to his anxiety. "Thou shalt not bear false witness. Thou shalt not steal. Thou shalt not kill."

He had become part of a brotherhood, however, and owed it to his companions-in-arms to defend them. He mustn't let them down because of his moral squeamishness. But could he kill a man? A Union soldier could be Junior, his own brother. A neighbor from a farm along New River. Marcus prayed he wouldn't have to kill, but he was equipped and willing to fight for his own life. He owed his family and Maylene that. And he owed his fellow soldiers whatever was required to keep them alive.

Marcus became increasingly edgy and slept poorly. He tried to shut out the ache of homesickness, his anxiety about Maylene. He concluded he should have married her before he left. He'd heard Amos had enlisted the year before, but there might be other Amos Wallaces passing through. Maylene wasn't the sort of girl to go unnoticed. He knew she intended to wait for him, but three years? No, the war couldn't possibly last that long.

He wrote letters home, but it was impossible to receive them. The company was on the move too much and the secrecy of their movements was vital. Their captain promised they'd be able to collect mail when they settled in their winter camp, wherever that might be.

My dear Maylene,

I'm missing you something terrible. I ate those johnnycakes and eggs the first day. I knew you wouldn't mind me not sharing them.

I see Corbin near every day. I know he writes, but tell Mary he's fine. He talks about her and little Robbie all the time.

I miss Mama's cooking, too. The food is nothing you'd care to eat. But I'm getting along all right, and I think of you every day. I wish I was home fixing up the cabin for us. Papa said he's going to work on the furniture this winter. That will spare me some work when I get home.

You mustn't worry yourself about those Union fellers up on Flat Top. We got word they was called back east to cause trouble at Richmond. I've a feeling they'll be the ones with trouble on their hands if they do.

Stay well and out of trouble as best you can.

Your loving,

Marcus

Maylene found it strange the way so many things stayed the same with Marcus gone. As usual, a sparrow pair nested in a cedar by the barn. The sheared sheep grew back their heavy wool. The corn went to tassel, then grew plump, fragrant ears. Papa's hoe could be heard scraping in the garden. She helped stack hay. She labored at the washboard. She milked the cow and churned butter.

Fall came, and the trees put on their vibrant colors. Extra quilts went on the beds. Callouses sloughed off her soles when she returned her bare feet to shoes. Flocks of ducks stopped at the river on their way south. Brightly feathered songbirds—warblers, orioles, tanagers—disappeared unnoticed, like ghosts passing through walls.

Maylene read and re-read every letter, impatiently waiting for one with a return address so she could reply.

There had been two arrivals since Marcus's departure—Mary had moved back home, and with her was Robbie, now a toddler on the brink of walking. With blond curls and blue eyes, he looked much like Papa, and Maylene was glad her father finally had a boy in the household again. Another baby was on the way, making Mary ravenous.

"You'll eat us out of house and home. How did Corbin feed you?" Maylene asked.

"You'll see what it's like," Mary answered through a mouthful of cornbread with honey. "I get so hungry I feel like chewing my own fingers."

"Does it hurt to have your belly swell like a melon?"

"No, silly, but I had backaches toward the end with Robbie. Corbin could tell you I fussed a bit."

Mary smiled before taking her next bite and Maylene took in her wide mouth, slight overbite, dimpled chin, and Farley-blue eyes. She might not be a classic beauty, but there was something so disarmingly welcoming about Mary's face and personality Maylene was not surprised Corbin had fallen hard for her.

Maylene wanted to ask more, about how it was to make a baby in the first place, but certain topics were too awkward to approach, even with a sister, and this one topped the list. Like Marcus, she knew the most basic aspects of anatomy and function, but a great deal was left to her imagination.

Maylene's inner life fluctuated between fantasies of her life with Marcus when he returned and anticipation of losing him. Although she tried to lose herself in the former, images of the latter stalked her, especially at night. At length, she would roll onto her back, clasp her hands beneath her breasts, and pray fervently, begging God to let Marcus live, until sleep overtook her.

There was a devastating change in the Lilly household that fall. The Confederate draft age was raised to forty-five. Quentin Lilly, at forty-three, received notice. With Pal being too necessary for the farm and the mule being too old, the cavalry was not an option. Quentin might have tried to buy a horse, but he and Suzanne were putting aside every dollar they could in the hope that Johnny could purchase a mount when his time came. They wanted him to serve with Marcus, closer to home.

By October Quentin was in uniform, training with the 36th Virginia Infantry. While his wife kept her anguish to herself, his children were bereft.

My dear Maylene,

I'm not supposed to say where we are, but it's somewhere you'd like to see. It feels like no white man has ever been here and looks like the trees have never known axe or saw. I've rarely seen such giants.

By now you've heard about the action at Fayetteville. We did advance scouting to secure the Turnpike, but didn't go as far as F-ville. Those Rebs of Loring's had a fine time of it, chasing the Yanks all the way to Charleston!

We drove some blue coat scouts helter skelter up a mountain last week and took their horses. Those boys didn't run upslope so well, tripping and cussing. I figured them for flatlanders and would have laughed if the Captain hadn't been nearby taking it all so serious. The two we took prisoner wee Lester could have run down without half trying. They was plumb winded.

I wish I could write more, but it's so far from here to the nearest Post—they say it's sixteen miles, and hard ones at that—we are getting only one chance at it from here.

Have you gotten your wood split for the winter? Have you killed the hog yet? I could sure use some bacon and sausage about now. Don't be eating all the fatback! I'll be wanting some when I get home.

I don't mean to write about food, but we all talk about it a fair bit. I didn't expect to miss it so much.

Much more, I miss you. I hope this finds you well and happy. You mustn't miss me too much. You'll have plenty of time with me around, maybe too much! You'll be asking me if I don't have another war to go off to.

I am well as can be, so don't worry a minute. Tell your ma and pa and sisters I send my hello.

Imagine I'm tucking you in tonight with a kiss. Will that keep you awake? It will me.

Your loving,

Marcus.

Winter camp came just in time, or so Marcus thought. By then his nerves were as taut as a colt's on a windy day. He'd been fired upon and he'd fired back. He knew he'd wounded a man, possibly killed him. The Rangers had been ambushed more than once. There had been skirmishes. A picket had been killed by a sniper at night. The game they played had become increasingly deadly, with mounting stakes on both sides.

Marcus didn't believe he could withstand the sights and sounds of slaughter on the battlefields, which were more often chaotic woods exploding with ordnance and smothered in smoke than open fields of comprehensible advances and retreats. Yet the insidious nature of mountain bushwhacking and espionage didn't allow for times of rest in camp, no real lulls between storms. Danger lurked behind every tree and boulder. Any sharp sound could be a rifle barrel steadied against a rock. The flash of light through leaves could be a gleaming bayonet, a sword. Any stranger, anyone without credentials was unworthy of trust and must be deemed a potential enemy.

Vigilance was required at all times, and it was nothing like the measured vigilance of the hunter. Marcus had learned what it is to be hunted.

My dear Marcus,

I thought I'd never be able to write! I trust you are housed for the winter and shall get this letter. I have loved getting yours and don't know how I would have gotten through the past seven months without them. Everyone is well here, and your family too. We heard that Junior was taken prisoner, and we pray for him every day. Papa said your ma has written you about Junior, or I wouldn't say. We pray for your pa too.

Mama's brother George was killed at Sharpsburg and she took the news hard. It's not that she's crying, she's just so mad. You never seen her like this, slamming pans onto the stove and cussing. And you know she how she feels about cussing. She says she don't even know who to be mad at, and she don't want to hear none of Papa's talk about forgiveness. Papa said all right. She dyed her meeting dress black in the wash tub. I grieve for my little cousins in Charlottesville.

We had our first snow last week, but not much. I hope you are able to keep warm. Has the food gotten better? They should feed you better in winter!

I worry about you but you are a Lilly, which means you are tough as nails.

Do you remember any of the stories we used to make up? I wish I remembered better. When you get home, I want you to tell me a new one. Will you? I been trying to make one up for you, but I need your help—your imagination is wilder than mine.

Mary's baby will be here soon—she is as big as a barn (but don't tell her I said so). Tell Corbin she is well and eating everything in sight. Robbie is as cute as he can be and we all love him to pieces. I think Papa is relieved to have a boy in the house.

What will you do in camp all winter? I see no point in drilling all day. If they don't keep you busy, they should send you home.

As for me, I'm busy with all the usual chores. The crops and garden done well this year. But I'm sure it's not a kindness to tell you that! I didn't have a chance to look for persimmons, but it wouldn't have been the same without you. Melva is sick with a cough, so I'm doing some of her chores, too. Do you think she's in bed with a book?

We pray every day for the war to end. We heard Buddy Adkins was killed.

We are still under martial law, but we hear this western part of the state may break away and become a new state. There is such turmoil.

Have you ever seen such a disorganized letter? Mr. Harvey would make me start over and re-write the whole thing.

No, I don't believe I shall ever wish to send you away to another war. One is more than enough.

Marcus you feel so far away but I hold you close in my heart. Come home to me.

Your loving,
Maylene

The men had begun felling trees, digging fire pits, and assembling rough chimneys in mid-November. They constructed crude huts that made Marcus's unfinished cabin seem a palace in comparison.

The respite Marcus needed was not to be, however. With the exception of the coldest and snowiest weeks of winter, scouting trips continued to be organized. Supplies ran low. Confiscation was required when goods weren't volunteered, Union sympathizers being prime targets. Illnesses spread through camp—bronchitis, pneumonia. Two died. Tempers were known to flare and fights broke out.

Along with the rest, Marcus took his two-hour picket duties. It became routine to stand at his post in the cold, his loaded rifle in hand, studying constellations crisp and close in the winter sky, Orion, Gemini.

One late-December night he listened to a distant great-horned owl giving its soft hoots. A sound to his side made him snap his head around. A bullet whined past his right ear. Marcus threw himself to the ground, raised his rifle and fired, blindly. He half-saw, half-intuited movement behind trees, heard running footsteps in the darkness, a shout from a nearby picket. Then the galloping cadence of a horse's hooves.

Local bushwhacker, he thought, already beginning to reload his gun, hating that his hands shook.

There was no chase. It was pointless in the dark, over unfamiliar terrain. But the Rangers would make inquiries. Someone's house might be burned, horses stolen. Captain Thurmond wasn't known for taking insults lightly.

During the weeks that followed, Marcus sought to distract himself by creating the story Maylene had requested but found the task beyond him. His mind thrashed about, unable to rest on a single thread of thought and follow it in a consistent direction. All was twists and turns.

I shan't return a madman.

He took solace in the only fantasy that could hold him, carry him away from the daily tedium, anxiety, cold, hunger, and homesickness of the hard-fisted winter. He would undress Maylene and take her to bed in their cabin on the mountainside under stars that hung in a silent sky above Broomstraw Ridge, above the Lilly farm with its little run meandering its way to Madam's Creek, sliding brightly, unhurried, for the New.

CHAPTER SEVEN

My darling Marcus,

I'm sure your family has written about the burning of Jumping Branch, but I wanted to wait until I saw the wreckage. Papa saw the federal troops when they had completed the Ferry crossing and begun making their way up the mountain. He said there must have been more than a thousand. No doubt you heard Bluestone Baptist was destroyed, along with the store and nearby homes. The mill was badly damaged. Some say the Yanks were looking for Mr. Jeff Bennett's home, suspecting him of foul play, and burned the village when no one would say where he lives. But why on Earth would somebody burn down a church? I suppose it was seen as a gathering place of Rebels—that's the only sense I can make of it and small sense it is. We are grateful to Mr. Meador for continuing to handle mail out of his cousin's home which was spared. Folks are so beat down, fearful that rebuilding will only result in a second attack. Mr. Harvey says they should wait until the war ends, but who knows how long that may be. For a while grain had to be carried from Jumping Branch and Broomstraw all the way to Madam's Creek, and you know how our Charlton Mill don't run much of the summer with the water so low. So some went on to Richmond's.

After the attack, Papa forbade us to go anywhere except church, but Melva and I finally sweet talked him into a trip to Jumping Branch last week and we just about cried when we got there. It's a sorry sight, let me tell you, with houses burned right down to their foundations and trees turned into black skeletons. Melva said she hated the Yankees for what they done. But you know Papa. He said we'd best remember the war will end and the time will come for mending fences. He said don't you girls be carrying hatred in your hearts. And he said many of those boys must have hated what they done, but they had no choice. I have my doubts about that, but I let Papa have his say. Melva just rolled her eyes—you know how she does.

I can tell you anyone who wishes you harm is my sworn enemy, and I would fight beside you if I could. Annie Plumley told Melva there are women dressed up like men who sneaked into the army, but I don't believe it. That would take more than a uniform and a haircut to pull off! But if there was a way to be with you, I would rather endure hardships and danger than be here missing you. I ache so bad for you sometimes I can't hardly breathe.

I pray this finds you warm and well.

Your loving intended,

Maylene

My dear Maylene,

Two flocks of robins come through this past week and the horses are starting to shed a little. So spring can't be far away and we'll be on the move again before long. I'd best get this letter out while I have the chance.

Winter felt mighty long in camp with all these men, out of sorts every one. We are all homesick, hungry, and tired of the sight and smell of one another. I go hunting every chance I get, just to be away from camp. But game is scarce and I have to go farther each time for as much as a rabbit.

Did your Grandma send another novel for your birthday? I know you'll save it for me if she did. The only thing I get to read anymore is a newspaper, and not very often. Soon the papers will be full of campaign accounts again, and we can hope the South shall prevail and this weary war shall end this year! It has about wore me out.

Know that I miss you and think of you every day. I would write much more often if I could. Your letters this winter have meant the whole world to me. I must have them all just about memorized by now.

Your loving,

Marcus

It was a March evening when winter had entirely exhausted its welcome. The girls' pa had taken the lantern to the barn for the purpose of milking. Melva had placed a candle on the small table between two high-backed willow chairs in front of the fireplace, her nose in a novel. A faint crease formed between her eyes as she got down to the pleasure of focused reading. With needle, thread, patch, and pants, Maylene took the adjacent chair. She intended to mend her father's spare pair of trousers, already on its second set of knee patches. Before setting to work, she slid the iron candleholder closer, to the middle of the table.

"I can't see," said Melva, looking up. She moved the candle back to its previous place.

Maylene felt like pointing out that her mending work was more important that her sister's recreation, but instead she sighed as loudly as she could and got up to fetch another candle from the chest by the door. There she found the wooden candle box empty. How had they gotten down to their last candle with no one noticing? She suspected Melva of failing to report the spent supply.

Maylene didn't quite slam the chest lid, but she let it speak. "We're out of candles—we'll have to share that one."

Melva ignored her.

Maylene retook her seat and shoved the candleholder back in her direction.

Moments later, Melva's head snapped up. "How am I supposed to read with you hogging the light?" She moved the candle so quickly she nearly extinguished the flame.

Before she could stop herself, Maylene jumped to her feet, picked up the coveted light and said with rising volume, "Melva, you are only reading a book and that one at least twice already. I am trying to fix Papa's pants. Now you tell me which matters more. I am sick and tired of you insisting on getting your way."

"Give me that!" Melva was on her feet.

Maylene held the candleholder high above her head and took a step back. "Just try and take it from me—I dare you!"

Margaret, seated on a stool, had paused in her spinning to watch the theatrics. "Hold your ground, Maylene. Watch the wax!"

Maylene felt the burn inflicted by molten beeswax on her hand and turned her head, hastily straightening the candle. "Ow!"

Melva took advantage and lunged, grabbing Maylene's raised wrist.

"Let go!" Maylene shouted, shoving her free hand against her sister's face.

Mary, who had been knitting at the table, erupted in a fit of laughter. Margaret doubled over with a squeal of glee.

Across from Mary, with Robbie on her lap, sat a stunned Sara Mae. "Girls!"

She was gearing up for a scalding parental rebuke when the candle and holder crashed to the floor, snuffing the flame, breaking the candle, and scattering liquified wax.

"Look what you done!" Maylene yelled.

"What *I* done!"

Melva looked down at the mess and then at her mother. She turned burning blue eyes on Maylene and then spun away, abruptly subdued.

Maylene knew what awaited her. The searing anger withdrew as quickly as it had engulfed her. She had to absorb the same punishment that had silenced her sister, her mother's rare look. And there it was. The look that said I am so ashamed of you I have no words to express this degree of disappointment.

"I'm sorry, Mama," Maylene said in a near-whisper. "I'll take care of this."

Dear Marcus,

I confess to being out of sorts, too. Missing you and being cooped up with my sisters is a perfect recipe for quarrels. I've done bitten my tongue nearly in half! But I confess I lost my temper with Melva last night, and over a trifling thing. I won't bother you with it, but it had to do with a shortage of candlelight, and one wanting to read and the other sew. I shall get busy making new candles this day!

It's fortunate Papa missed our little spat—you know how he hates to see us fight—although Mary and Margaret appeared well entertained. Mama gave us such a look of disgust I was quite ashamed. I am even more ashamed to write of such a thing when you are suffering God only knows what hardships. You can see I can't even think of something worthwhile to tell you.

So let me say simply that I love you with my whole heart and know when you are near I am not inclined to fuss at anyone because I am happy. I fear I shall never become used to your absence. I wish I were more like Mary. She says her prayers and goes right to sleep, as though she hasn't a care in the world, while I toss and turn like a fevered child.

Stay as warm and well as you possibly can, and tell your Captain you must have a furlough before the Farley girls come to blows.

With love and longing, and concern this letter is going out too late to find you,

Your Maylene.

Spring of 1863 found the company in reasonable health and itching to be on the move. The men packed the mules, saddled the horses, and resumed their nomadic life.

Within days, Marcus fell ill. He had never been truly sick before, nothing more than sniffles. He dropped like a stone in a well. Typhoid fever.

The company had no means of caring for him. They were passing by the village of Oak Hill and found an aging widow, Mrs. Kirk, willing to take in him and another ailing soldier. The dear woman did her best to keep Marcus warm on the cold spring nights, as he shivered and coughed uncontrollably. His head ached. His fever raged out of control, and he fell into a confused stupor, unaware of the splotchy rash that crept ominously across his torso.

Corbin checked on him before the Rangers moved on, arriving as the town physician was leaving the weathered frame home. The doctor, elderly and stooped in a dark suit, reported, "Private Young is recovering from pneumonia. The other— that's one sick soldier."

"Let's not speak of him as a soldier, sir," Corbin cautioned.

"As you wish." The doctor sounded impatient. "I don't expect him to resume his duties."

"You expect him to die?"

"I consider it likely."

Marcus was seized by severe abdominal pains that yanked him out of his near-catatonia.

Tough as nails. He repeated Maylene's words before sliding back into oblivion.

The widow spooned soup broth down his parched throat whenever he woke.

Dimly, Marcus wondered who she was and thought he should thank her, but sleep dragged him under again. He dreamed of blazing colors and looming shapes that made him feel miniaturized and vulnerable. He thought he was basking in the creek at home and woke to find his bedding and undergarments soaked through. He felt his flesh was becoming a rotting slippery Jack, a mushroom with pores in place of gills. He could smell the decay.

It would have been a comfort to give up the fight and slip away. To lift into the sky and be done with the misery wracking his body, be done with the war. But Maylene. He had told her he would come home.

Tough as nails…. Maylene.

His energy was entirely gone.

I'm sorry.

He succumbed again.

A neighboring couple—fellow members of Mrs. Kirk's Baptist congregation—began to assist. They had two conscripted sons and said they'd want someone to do the same for their boys should they fall ill. Charles and Bertha Hill helped Marcus use the chamber pot, although he was too dehydrated and food-deprived to have much use for it. They rolled him over and checked for bed sores as they wrestled a soiled bed pad out from under him. They took home quilts to wash and offered fresh ones. And they watched with anxious eyes as Marcus turned into a skeleton, a skeleton with an alarmingly distended belly. The swelling resolved itself in explosive diarrhea that elevated the Hills to sainthood in Mrs. Kirk's estimation. Marcus was mercifully dazed beyond embarrassment. He knew only the sensation of hands and damp rags on his skin, and murmuring voices that made no sense.

Three weeks after Marcus arrived, the widow noticed a change. She had nursed enough children through illness to know a healing sleep. She touched his cheek, cooler.

Son of a gun, this boy is going to live, she thought before backing out of the room, closing the door without a breath of sound.

A week later, Marcus was making wobbly trips to the outhouse. On his next visit, the doctor announced his patient was well enough to travel by wagon. Marcus might as well go home. It would likely be several months before he could rejoin his company.

A little money had been left for his care and burial. Mrs. Kirk refused payment and insisted the funds be used to hire a Negro instructed to fetch lumber from a mill near New Richmond, a full-day's distance away. Not that it was necessary to travel that far for lumber. Dressed in civilian clothes and wrapped in a blanket, Marcus lay in the wagon on a cushion of straw, occasionally joining the driver for brief spells on the seat. Astonished by his weakness, he grew light-headed and faintly nauseated while upright, soon returning to the wagon bed. It was hard to believe he was going home. He'd have been excited, had he the energy.

At New Richmond, a willing boy was dispatched to the Radcliff farm. Corbin's white-bearded father, Ben, arrived on horseback an hour later, then walked back home leading the horse, with Marcus woozily mounted. The next day Ben and Marcus made their way across New River on the ferry and continued to the Richmond farm in search of a spare horse. Having secured a mare, Marcus willed himself up the New, past the mill and mist-spewing thunder of Richmond's Falls, the whitewater chaos of Brooks Falls, nine winding miles to Madam's Creek. Muddle-headed, exhausted, and smiling, he arrived at the Farley farm by the middle of the afternoon.

CHAPTER EIGHT

Maylene was hoeing a row of potatoes when she saw Dolly and Spit lift their heads from grazing. They trotted toward the fence. An unfamiliar horse was crossing the bridge, approaching the cabin.

Who on earth... It can't be. Oh, God, let it be.

There was no mistaking. Even pale as a moth and skeletally thin, the man approaching was unquestionably her Marcus. She dropped the hoe and began to run.

Sara Mae, hearing hoofbeats on the bridge, stepped out the door and then back inside, abruptly teary. "An answer to our prayers," she said, wiping an eye with her apron skirt.

Mary, who was nursing Sallie Mae on a porch rocker, gathered her baby and followed her mother inside.

Marcus had to lean against the horse after dismounting. Had he not, Maylene would have knocked him flat.

After a meal and a rest, Marcus continued home. Maylene wanted to go with him, but Papa was firm.

"Give him a bit with his family, honey. You can't go barging in like a loose bull."

Her father rode up with her the next day. Maylene didn't say so, but she hoped to stay and have Papa take both mules home, along with the Richmond's borrowed mare.

Suzanne had already considered the matter. Marcus remained in need of care—if Maylene wanted to stay, she was welcome. The little boys were moved to the boys' room upstairs, Marcus into their room. Maylene crowded in with the four sisters, who were bubbling over with excitement and took her in as one of their own.

Marcus fell headlong into the feather down of a family and fiancé intent on loving him back to health.

A few weeks later, Pastor Mullens told the congregation about a three-day revival the following week, up at Rhoda Ann Church on Spicelick Run. Marcus felt ready for an outing and suggested he and Maylene ride Pal up the back way, the path they took up Broomstraw as kids. It was the shortcut to Jumping Branch, a steep route but only three miles from the Lilly farm. From Jumping Branch it was a few rolling miles to where the little church crouched on the edge of Spicelick, overlooking one of the best swimming holes in the area.

Suzanne said, "Take one of the girls along. It don't look right, you going alone."

Johnny countered, "Ma, they're grown up and betrothed and don't need no chaperone. If you can't trust Marcus, you can't trust no one."

They went alone, bareback, on Pal. It was a perfect late-May day, with swallows pirouetting over the pastures and a goldfinch singing from the uppermost branch of a dead locust. Maylene put her arms around Marcus's too-narrow waist to keep from sliding backwards on Pal's broad back as the horse picked his way upward. Sitting sideways had always struck her as absurd. As soon as they were in the woods and out of sight, she straddled Pal and nuzzled Marcus's neck.

"We'll have to ride back for a chaperone if you keep that up," scolded Marcus.

Maylene laughed, but she stopped the nuzzling. It occurred to her it was the first time she had felt truly happy and relaxed in over a year.

Marcus, too, was in fine form—singing, pointing out a flycatcher nest she would never have seen, patting Maylene's knee for emphasis as he talked. They dallied, stopping to take in the view when they reached the top of the ridge.

By the time they got to the church, the meeting was in recess for lunch. They shared the cornbread, dried apples, and beef jerky they'd brought along. Then Marcus stripped off his shirt, snatched a rope hung over a sycamore branch, and sailed out over the water. In he plunged, joining several splashing children. As he climbed out for another turn on the rope, Maylene could count every rib.

A shadow passed over her. She wanted him to be wholly well again, and yet she did not. A healthy Marcus was a Marcus doomed to soldier on in the war that seemed to have no end.

After drying in the sun for a spell, Marcus slipped back into his shirt. A balding man in suspenders announced the meeting would resume in a few minutes.

"Let's get out of here," Marcus said.

"Why?"

"I can't kiss you here."

They stopped again at the crest of Broomstraw Ridge, Maylene resting her head on Marcus's shoulder.

With Maylene, Marcus was finding himself again. He was well enough to feel the flow of blood to every extremity, and a renewed vigor in his hands.

"Let's get married next Sunday. That gives me a whole week to make a door," he said without warning.

Maylene let her body collapse against Marcus's frail form. She tightened her grip around his waist. She put her mouth close to his ear, which made Marcus want to pull her from Pal's back and take her right then, even if he didn't know exactly what to do.

"Next Sunday, as in eight days?" she murmured.

"Eight days seems too long."

"Think how strong you'll be by then."

"Does that mean yes?"

"Yes."

Having reached the treetops, the sun perched on the horizon like an overfed nestling. As they came out of the woods, Marcus and Maylene noticed two saddled horses tied to the porch rail of the Lilly home. Marcus peeled himself off Pal's sweat-sticky back, helped Maylene down, slipped off the bridle, and turned the horse into the paddock. Corbin and a stranger stepped out of the house, onto the porch.

"Good to see you looking better than dead, Marcus," Corbin said.

Marcus reached for the outstretched hand. "Who says I ain't?"

"This here is Doc Perkins, from Mercer County. We been camped near Princeton, and I been sent up to do some scouting for recruits. Thought we'd stop by and check on you."

Marcus took Dr. Perkins' hand. "Pleased to meet you. This is Miss Farley, my intended." There was no mistaking the pride in his voice.

The doctor gave Marcus a sidelong look before taking him inside for a hasty exam. Once completed, Marcus came back outside, buttoning his shirt. Dr. Perkins followed with his bag of instruments.

"Give yourself another fortnight, son. I'd like to see you put a little more weight on."

"Yes, sir. I'll see what I can do."

Maylene, having risen from a rocker, blanched and felt her knees weaken. She looked away, her eyes finding a thunderhead, crowned with the day's last light, towering over Broomstraw Ridge. As she watched, it slipped into shadow, taking the day's happiness with it into the dusk.

CHAPTER NINE

The door was a stout and handsome work of chestnut. At a lower corner, on the inside, Marcus carved a small heart, within which he etched M + M. He wondered how long it would be before it caught Maylene's eye.

The night before the wedding, Maylene was such a bundle of nerves she abandoned her sewing and took the churn out on the porch. There she began furiously turning the day's cream into butter.

Sara Mae gathered up the discarded dress and joined her daughter outside, choosing the rocker. "There's some things I should tell you."

"Like what?" Standing at the churn, Maylene didn't look up. She guessed what was coming.

"About your wedding night." Sara Mae focused on needle and thread. "You know your papa took fright when he learned we was heading back to Charlottesville and he proposed. We could have married right then, but it was too close on the heels of Melvin's death, and I wanted to wait for spring. We thought May. So I moved in with my friend Ethel Hatcher's family.

"I know. Up Beech Run."

"Yes, that's the Harvey farm now. Well, we got impatient and moved the date up to March. But the weather turned bad, and my ma and pa got only as far as Lexington before they had to turn back...."

Maylene waited.

"So your grandma never had this little talk with me, and our wedding night was... it was a bit of a shock to me."

"What happened?" Maylene looked at her mother.

Sara Mae laughed. "Nothing terrible. It was just that I didn't know what to expect. Do you?"

"Not entirely."

"Well, honey, you know how a rooster mounts a hen and a boar mounts a sow when they mate. A man and woman have to... come together, too, to create life."

"I know that much."

"I reckon you do. But it's different. We come together face to face, with much kissing. It can be very romantic and sweet."

Maylene continued raising and lowering the dash with notable vigor. She could think of nothing to add or ask without extreme embarrassment.

Sara Mae looked up from her sewing, as if searching the farm for the right words. "A man's organ has to enter you to pass his seed. But the first time or two, there may be some discomfort."

Maylene felt the alarm of rising flood waters roiling inside. Discomfort? What sort of discomfort?

"And you may bleed a little. It's perfectly natural."

Bleed? Natural? What could be natural about hurting and bleeding? Maylene was beginning to wish her mother had stayed inside and never brought up this awful subject.

"Oh," she said, trying to sound nonchalant.

"But after a time or two... it's...pleasant."

"It is?"

"Oh, honey, you'll see. God intends it to be pleasant, I do believe. Just give yourself time and don't be fretful. Marcus loves you and shall do his best to be gentle and kind."

Is that before or after he hurts me and makes me bleed?
"I know.... Can we talk about something else now?"
Sara Mae exhaled audibly. "Anything at all."

It was left to Suzanne to talk to Marcus, and she approached
the duty with reluctance. She found him resting between tasks,
stretched out on his bed.

"Don't get up. I won't be here but a minute," she said as he
sat up, yawning. She seated herself next to her son.

"It pains me your pa and Junior aren't here to see you wed.
Your pa would be mighty proud and happy. The day you and
Maylene came down to the house with your big news, he said,
'I've always thought that girl's as smart as she is pretty. And
she don't have a mean bone in her body. The Farleys are good
people.'"

"He said all that?"

"He did, and I agreed. You've chosen well, Marcus. I fully
trust you'll never have reason to regret your choice. And the
Good Lord willing, you'll come home from this war and have
many years together. I believe with all my heart you'll be a
husband who shall make me proud."

Marcus, unaccustomed to praise from his mother, smiled
broadly. "I'll do my best."

"Now, as for your wedding night," Suzanne continued,
"you'll do what comes natural. But see to it you don't act like a
wild beast and scare that poor girl half to death."

With that, she rose to her feet.

Marcus's smile evaporated. "Yes, ma'am."

"Do you have any questions before I go?"

"I don't reckon so."

Suzanne left him alone. Marcus collapsed onto his back, unable
to nap, worried about the unknown beast that might emerge and
uncomfortably curious about his parents' wedding night.

They married that seventh of June at the Baptist church on Madam's Creek, Pastor Mullens presiding. Marcus naively thought Maylene would attend the morning service and was briefly panicked by her absence.

Making his way down the aisle to his seat, Bob Farley squeezed Marcus's shoulder. "Don't worry, son, she'll be along. She's prettying up this morning."

The next hour was one of the longest in his memory, and Marcus fervently hoped it would be the last time he endured a sermon futilely trying to subdue romantic—and not particularly holy—thoughts about Maylene, along with their physical effects. His prayers for patience served no end. Marcus sweated, fidgeted, and fantasized his way through the endless service.

Most of the small congregation stayed for the brief ceremony. With so much bad news wearing on its members, the little community welcomed a cause for celebration. Maylene, with her mother's help, had time and means to do no more than add fresh lace to the newest dress among the sisters. It was the yellow dress she had made for Margaret. She looked to Marcus like the Sun itself entering the little chapel on her papa's arm.

A jovial caravan—made up of some on foot, some on horseback, a few in buggies or carts—followed the newlyweds to the Farley farm, where a sumptuous picnic ensued. Maylene scarcely ate and Marcus didn't fare much better. The most striking feature was basket upon basket of strawberries provided by hosts and guests alike. Sara Mae put out two pitchers of cream. There wasn't one who completed the meal without red-stained fingers.

As the day wore on, Marcus resumed his prayers, asking God to make the guests leave. Maylene stifled yawns, having slept little the night before. Shadows were long by the time the last departed and the Lillys—all on foot except for Marcus and Maylene triumphantly atop Pal—headed up the hollow.

It was a nervous but eager Marcus who turned the horse into the pasture and led Maylene by the hand for the uphill walk to the waiting cabin, outfitted with table, benches, and the bed Johnny had made the previous winter. Their way was lit by countless fireflies and a sky ablaze with stars, as if Nature herself bejeweled their wedding night.

Maylene had a bad case of jitters, her hands shaking as she unbuttoned the bodice of her dress, her back to Marcus. She turned around to find him sitting on the bed, shirt off, pants on. His face was grave.

"It'll near kill me if I hurt or scare you," he said in a husky whisper.

"You shan't."

She lowered herself onto his lap, and the magic of attraction, amplified by years of closeness, snuffed out their fears like a flame before a torrent.

There they spent the next nine days, primarily in the new bed, filling in the gaps in their knowledge of each other's bodies, exploring the carnal mysteries they had long pondered. They slipped out for meals with the Lilly family, putting up with Johnny's smirks, yet despite Suzanne's best efforts, Marcus was able to gain no more than a pound or two. He was undoubtedly more active than the doctor would have advised.

Maylene took to Marcus in a way she could never have imagined. Having quickly reached and sprinted past "pleasant," she couldn't get her fill of him.

"Do you have a story for me?" she asked late one night.

"No. I have something better." He rolled on top of her and she shrieked with laughter.

Pal lifted his head, a mouthful of grass dangling, and swung it toward the cabin.

The temptation was too much for Johnny. Nearly a week into the honeymoon, when Marcus and Maylene arrived late and disheveled for breakfast, he said, "I trust the bed is proving worthy of the demands placed upon it."

"Johnny!" Suzanne exclaimed.

Calvin gave a snort of laughter but squelched his mirth at once, having picked up a clear message from his mother's withering look.

"It's a fine piece of furniture. Why don't you have another griddle cake?" For Maylene's sake, Marcus was doing his best to remain unruffled and occupy Johnny's mouth with anything other than words.

Eliza and Rachel exchanged looks and burst out laughing. "Girls!"

Their mother's disapproval wasn't enough to stem their flow of hilarity, but it was enough to send them out of the room. Maylene saw Rachel double over and clap a hand over her mouth as she reached the porch.

"What's so funny?" That was Lester.

"Not a thing. Eat your breakfast," answered his mother.

Louella studied her scrambled eggs with great interest. Vesta was mesmerized by the color of Maylene's face.

Marcus, meanwhile, had slid a bare heel overtop of his brother's toes and was pressing down with all his might. Smiling, Johnny retrieved his slightly flattened digits.

"We'll have no more such talk at this table. Am I understood?" Suzanne wasn't smiling.

"Yes, ma'am." Johnny beamed.

"Why don't you wipe that silly grin off your face and take a shot at acting proper?" Suzanne fired at him.

"Yes, ma'am." The grin remained.

Maylene met Johnny's eyes before looking back at her plate. She wanted him to know she wasn't mad. She felt Marcus squeeze her thigh in apology and knew he was making a herculean effort to maintain his composure. The poor man could scarcely swallow. A surge of love for the brothers struck her so forcefully an obstruction rose in her own throat. Her next swallow felt like a whole hard-boiled egg going down.

No one was mad at Johnny, not even his mother, for all her bluster. At this particular time, he could be forgiven almost anything.

John Samuel Lilly had turned eighteen on the first of June. On the sixteenth, a rider came up Madam's Creek after dark leading two horses—one black, one dun. Marcus and Johnny were expecting him.

This time, the parting was unbearable. Marcus was grateful for the darkness, which masked his tears. Maylene sobbed. She was running for the empty cabin before the horses disappeared into the mist.

"Best to leave her be," said Suzanne.

Maylene threw herself across the bed, clutching the bunched-up comforter, and cried until nearly dawn. She had never cried herself to exhaustion.

The next day she moved back home.

Three days later, on the twentieth of June, 1863, the state of West Virginia entered the Union. No longer part of Virginia, Raleigh and surrounding counties, as perceived by the majority of their inhabitants, rested in enemy territory. Mail to any Confederate state ceased.

The last delivery of Confederate mail to Jumping Branch included an envelope from Richmond, addressed to Quentin D. Lilly, Esq. Its contents related Quentin D. Lilly, Jr., had died at the Confederate prison camp, Castle Thunder, Richmond, Virginia, June 6, 1863.

Thereby ended the Lilly luck.

CHAPTER TEN

Marcus was on a slow burn. If he had hated his forced participation in the war before, he despised it now.

Late that summer, a Raleigh County recruit brought news of Junior's death. Surrounded by Confederate troops, it was difficult for Marcus and Johnny to grieve for their brother. It wasn't that their fellow soldiers didn't understand their pain, it was that it was pain tainted with shame. To the others, Junior was a traitor, and had gotten what he deserved.

Marcus feared what his mother feared, and lay awake like her unable to shut out, that Junior had been the target of especially harsh treatment by virtue of being a Southerner. He couldn't have opened his mouth without revealing that fact.

Compounding Marcus's angst was Johnny's presence. They both felt less homesick with the other near, but that benefit was outweighed by an ever-present weight pressing down on Marcus, imposed by the responsibility he felt for keeping Johnny safe. Although he loved other members of his company as brothers, and told himself Johnny was no different, he couldn't fool himself. This was the brother he had hunted and fished with, gone to church with, joked with, quarreled with, fought for covers in a bed with, worked shoulder-to-shoulder in the fields with, explored the forbidden topic of sex with…. It was Johnny, and he had to watch his back. There was hardly a moment when he didn't know where Johnny was, whether ahead, behind, or on picket detail. When Johnny was too far away to recognize, Marcus knew him by his mount, his dun mare. In the rare event that Marcus lost track, his stomach tightened and he couldn't relax until he'd set eyes on his brother again.

Marcus and Johnny no longer talked about the bigger picture. There was little point. Union forces were seen as invaders, aggressors they wanted rid of. Yankees had no business in the South. The less tangible issues of states' rights and slavery were far less personal to Marcus and the other mountaineers, who didn't own slaves and had always functioned so independently it wasn't clear how the larger debate affected them. They and the women they'd left behind raised their food and children by their own sweat, muscle, and lost sleep, along with a Biblical faith that gave them optimism against all odds. They lived by the natural order of things, as God intended, and they took pride in their grit.

Of course slavery was wrong—any child could see that. Marcus sensed its end coming. As writers, clergy, and politicians raised more and more strident voices against it, surely the institution would fall of its own grotesque and unpopular weight. In time. But now the matter would be put to rest at extraordinary cost, or, if the South prevailed, the issue would brew like a vicious storm building unseen in the night, only to erupt in violence another day.

Pride, hatred, instinctive loyalties, perceived oppression, fear of economic and cultural collapse... How the fight started and what sustained it had become cloudy. Both sides were guilty of atrocities, all manner of wrongs. What Marcus knew best was daily discomfort and the nerve-fraying pushing, back and forth. Forays, retreats. Occasional skirmishes. Nothing of significance accomplished. Union supply units penetrating farther and farther south. Sudden death by violence. Slow death by festering wound. Death by exposure. Death by infectious disease. He was becoming numb to it all.

He felt trapped as a coon up a tree, as much a prisoner as Junior had been. He could desert the Confederacy and flirt with a firing squad. He could stay with his company and die any number of ways. He could go home and be drafted by the Union to face the same risks in a different uniform. The war might be nothing but nonsense, orchestrated by madmen, but loyalty mattered to him, and there was Johnny. Besides, who else could he trust but this motley assortment of men who had taken up arms together? There was no actual choice, he would wait it out. Without any glorious goal in sight, he would do his best to fight for the same elemental reasons the other men fought—to stay alive, to keep one another alive, and to eliminate the men who sought to kill them.

It would help if he could hear from Maylene.

That summer, Marcus and Johnny were part of a detail that captured a Federal wagon train, gleaning a bounty of food, guns, and ammunition. The ambush was a breathtaking success, catching the Yankees in the open and completely off-guard. They fled like rabbits. Rebel-yelling, the Rangers gave chase, hounding and scattering the Union troops before circling back for their spoils. In those adrenaline-filled minutes, galloping, shouting, laughing—their tension and tedium replaced with a shared euphoria of invincibility—there wasn't a man among them, not even Marcus, who wanted to be anywhere else on earth.

Meanwhile, General Averell's Union troops advanced down the bony fingers of the mountains of eastern West Virginia, into Pocahontas and Greenbrier Counties. West and south of Greenbrier waited Confederate-sympathetic Raleigh, Mercer, and Monroe Counties. Guerrilla tactics intensified, favoring those who knew the challenging landscape best.

On the larger canvas, horrific casualties played out across a vast geography—Vicksburg, Chancellorsville, Gettysburg. By now both governments had passed drafts, sucking ever more men into the cavernous maw of Hades.

One night that fall, Marcus girded himself with coffee and shouldered his rifle for picket duty. The Rangers were camped in a wooded valley next to a small creek, their few tents clustered in the floodplain. Many men lay shelter-less, cocooned in wool blankets. The cook-fire had burned down to dull embers, and clouds obscured moon and stars. It was a black night.

Marcus was positioned a quarter-mile above the camp, next to the stream. He had just tugged his sleeves down over his knuckles for warmth when he heard the faint crack of a breaking twig. He froze, lifted the rifle barrel into his left hand. Nothing. He eased forward, wishing for the eyes of a cat, listening.

Someone was there, he knew it. A breeze rustled leaves above him, but he was sure there was another sound, someone moving beyond a thin screen of alders. His pulse accelerated. He stopped again.

The clouds parted enough to reveal the face of the moon. Marcus picked up its reflection off two eyes, looking straight at him through the alders.

Before his brain knew he would do it, without raising the rifle above his waist, he fired. There was a brief thrashing sound, the snapping of breaking branches, then a soft but distinct thud.

I've killed a man, Marcus thought. He ran, bent over, for the cover of a tree trunk. There could be more than one.

Lord, forgive me. I hadn't a choice.

The two closest pickets came running. Shouts and curses sounded from camp as officers began barking orders and sleep-addled men prepared for an attack. Marcus sent a man back to relay the message that there was no advancing army—another lone bushwhacker was likely all the threat they faced.

Johnny, the first to arrive from camp, impetuous, carried a pine-knot torch. Marcus took the torch when he saw his brother's face in its light, but held it warily at arm's length.

Corporal Warren said, "Spread out," in a gravelly whisper. He and five other men flanked Marcus, creeping into the dense vegetation, shotguns at the ready.

"Over here." Marcus immediately felt absurd to whisper when the darting flame exposed his position like a kettle drum.

He shouldered his way through the tangle of alders, scanning the ground. And there lay his victim—in the weak circle of light was an eight-point buck, bleeding from a wound in its throat.

Johnny hooted and pounded Marcus on the back. "Nice shot, brother!"

Shouts of glee rose into the night sky. The men could already taste venison in their hungering mouths.

Although Marcus ate as heartily as the rest at their meat-heavy breakfast the next morning, he was uneasy about the shooting. Back home, he would have known it was a deer. The eyes were too large, too far apart, to be a man's. He had reacted out of fear so primal it shut down his reason. What else might he do when afraid?

CHAPTER ELEVEN

My dear husband,

I am so happy to finally write to you! Your ma got word a Lilly cousin—Josiah—was turning eighteen and enlisting with the Rangers, and she let us know. Papa is going to take this letter up to Josiah on Ellison Ridge tomorrow. I would ride with him but he forbids it. I hope the reason will make you glad—I am going to have a baby! Can you believe it? I expect him or her to arrive in mid-March, less than five months. I have been dying to tell you all this time. You mustn't worry yourself about me. Mama and Mary will help me, and I know I can bring this baby into the world just fine. It will be a Lilly baby, so it will be strong and healthy. I wish you could tell me what name you want. If it's a boy, I'm thinking Marcus Quentin. What do you think? Quentin Marcus? It's a shame we never talked about names, but I don't figure either of us had this in mind when you were home!

I hope you are well. It must be good to have Johnny with you. Tell him we all send our love, and we pray for your safety every day. Papa says he thinks the war will end early next year. You know I'm dying for you to be home.

Tell Corbin, too, we pray for him. Robbie and Sallie Mae are growing like weeds. Papa has taught Robbie to whistle like a bobwhite.

Being with you at our cabin seems like something I dreamed, but I can look at my changing shape and know it wasn't a dream. It helps me wait. I love our baby already.

Marcus, I miss you every minute of every day. I'm saving a thousand kisses for you. We won't forget how, will we?

Your loving wife,

Maylene

Margaret came to the barn as her father saddled Dolly, handing him a letter to add to his satchel. It was addressed to Johnny.

Upon receipt, Marcus read and re-read the unexpected letter with its momentous news. He folded it small and carried it with him from then on. Johnny made no mention of his.

Dear Maylene,

We are camped not far from the state line. I am paying a boy to take this letter to White Sulphur Springs and mail it there. I should not, but I had to find a way to write. I'm sorry it has taken a few weeks. You mustn't say anything about where this letter came from. Be sure to burn the envelope.

A baby! We are going to be parents?! I knew we could be, but somehow it didn't seem possible. Just knowing you are well was enough good news for one letter. This extra news is beyond good. I wish I could be home to rejoice with you.

I think Quentin Marcus for a boy. You will come up with a good name for a girl, I know. I'll add prayers for our baby's safe arrival to my nightly list. You must take specially good care of yourself.

I would tell you what we've been doing if I could, but it don't bear repeating. Know that I am well, that I think of you every day, and that I am counting the hours until either the war is over or I am discharged. We've been apart too long for a man to stand it.

Johnny is a fine soldier, and he would be glad to tell you that. I am worn out keeping him out of trouble. Tell Mary that Corbin is as well as a man can be. We both want to lay down our guns and be farmers again. Johnny, not yet! He's happy as a coon in a cornfield. He got named "Red Lilly" right away, which suits him fine. I'm the only one here calls him Johnny.

When the baby comes, give the little guy or gal a kiss from me. And say I'll be there as soon as I can.

Don't worry. I shall not forget how to kiss you.

Your loving,

Marcus

The cow was restless one night that November, and Bob Farley checked on her after midnight, thinking a bobcat or even a bear might be on the prowl. But he found nothing amiss in or around the log barn, and the cow quieted as soon as she heard his familiar voice.

"Quit yer bawling," he said, and shuffled back across the frosty grass to bed.

It was Maylene's turn to milk in the morning. Instantly evident was an oddity that brought the yawning milkmaid fully awake. The pale-brown cow showed no urgency for milking, and her udder lacked its usual bloated tautness. Baffled, Maylene, ran a hand along the bony bovine spine.

"What's wrong, my girl? Why…"

A sound behind her made her turn sharply. There was no mistaking—even in the dim dawn light—the barrel of a rifle she looked directly into. It was no more than three feet away and aimed at her face.

Maylene straightened with an involuntary yelp of fear. She took a step backward, raising an arm protectively and bumping into the cow.

"Be quiet!" hissed the holder of the gun. "I ain't planning to shoot you, but if you start hollering, I just might have to."

He was a thin, dark-haired boy in a gray uniform festooned with bits of straw. He stood outside the cow's stall, resting the rifle barrel on the top rail. Maylene guessed he couldn't be older than fourteen. His voice cracked with the uncertainty of the boy-man divide, and his body shook uncontrollably. Maylene wondered if it was fear, fever, or cold that made the boy tremble. The sharp edge of her fear softened slightly with pity.

"You run away."

"I got lost is all."

"You been drinking the milk."

The boy dropped his gaze.

"It's all right, I guess." That said, Maylene was at a complete loss as to what to do or say next. A lethal weapon remained pointed in her direction, although with less authority.

"Maybe you should talk to my pa," she ventured.

Immediately Maylene regretted those words. The boy raised the barrel menacingly. "I'm warning you, miss. You say anything about seeing me to anyone and someone's gonna get hurt."

"Then I won't…. But you need help, don't you?"

Maylene saw something collapse within the boy. He swallowed before he spoke again.

"Just need to sleep a little while and I'll be on my way. I'll be needing food."

"That can be arranged. Will you be warm enough in the straw?"

"Yes, ma'am."

"Then I'll leave you be. There's no one here wishes you harm. You can rest easy. Will you lower that gun, please?"

"Yes, ma'am."

Maylene saw the shine of tears in the exhausted boy's dark eyes as he pulled back the rifle with a gesture of resignation. She opened the stall gate, stepped gingerly around the boy-soldier, and left the barn.

Later that morning, Bob brought Dolly to the barn, stopping in the open doorway. He tied the mule to an iron ring imbedded in a timber, stepped inside for a curry comb, and came back out.

"Dolly, you contrary mule, if you'd quit wallerin' in the mud like a hog I wouldn't have to wear us both out scraping all this dirt offa you."

Bob began making circular motions with the toothed tool, sending skyward a cloud of dust. The fine particles rose lazily in the still air and caught on the farmer's heavy blond eyebrows.

"You're gonna choke me to death with this dust, you big fat ball a' filth. I have a mind to trade you in on a pair of hounds."

Bob worked his way around Dolly's rump and began scrubbing her back. In a louder voice, he said, "Ole girl, do you figure there's a young soldier nearby who can see I'm unarmed and might be willing to come out here and have a talk with me? I'm getting a little lonesome with no one to talk to but an old mule."

He continued his work, moving to Dolly's neck and raising a fresh plume of dust. The mule leaned into the curry comb, enjoying the scratching.

"That feels pretty good, don't it, Doll? Here, let me scratch up here behind your ears."

Bob had his back to the barn. By the time he ducked under Dolly's neck and began working on her near side, there was a boy standing in the doorway, in plain view.

"Well bless my sorry soul," Bob said, coming fully erect. "If you ain't the scrawniest soldier I ever laid eyes on. I've seen plucked poults with more meat on their bones."

He held out his hand. "Come here, son, and shake my hand. I don't bite. I'm Bob Farley and I intend to help you out if you'll let me."

The boy moved the rifle barrel to his left hand, stepped forward with sudden eagerness, and grasped the outstretched hand. Bob felt the tremor Maylene had described. Even his firm grip didn't squelch it.

"I'm much obliged, sir. I left my company in Virginia, and I'm... discharged. I'm heading home."

"And where would that be?"

"Lower Virginia, Wise County."

"I don't suppose you'll tell me your name."

"No, sir."

"You been following the river?"

"Yes, sir."

"Well, it won't get you to Wise County. It's time for you to part company with the New. You need to head back up a ways and pick up the Turnpike. Take it over White Oak Mountain to Glade Creek and then head south to Bluefield. From there, west. We can talk about it over some biscuits and gravy. That sound all right?"

"Yes, sir. I believe I know the way from Bluefield, and I believe I could use a biscuit."

The boy let Bob put an arm around his shoulders and lead him back to the cabin, leaving a partially de-caked Dolly dozing in the tepid sun.

After fortifying the lad with as much food as his stomach could hold and supplying him with a stash of boiled eggs and salted ham, Sara Mae was keen on getting the deserter out of her home.

But her husband said, "One more thing before you go. How long ago were you discharged?"

The boy counted on his tremulous fingers. "Been over a week by now."

Bob sat down at the table with a pencil and a page of paper torn from the ledger he used for keeping track of tax payments and any small income that found its way into his hands. He said, "I don't believe soldiering agreed with you, young man. Am I correct?"

"No, sir, I mean, yes, sir, that is correct. It was all right except for the fighting part."

Bob managed to maintain a poker face, but Maylene had to turn away to hide her smile. Sara Mae took interest in a pot that needed scrubbing, and Melva dropped her head over the rolling pin she pressed with renewed force into already-flattened dough. It was fortunate, Maylene thought, Mary was tending the baby upstairs, and Margaret and Robbie had been sent out for stove wood.

"I'm sure no one under this roof could endure the things you suffered," Bob said.

The boy looked confused, unsure if he was being insulted or praised. He shrugged.

"I'll call you James B. Jones if you don't mind," Bob said as he went to work.

Moments later, he rose and handed the finished note to the boy. "Son, you may have to swallow your pride and use this on occasion. I don't know if it'll work. And if anyone should figure out it's not exactly genuine, I'm asking you to return the favor of our hospitality by saying you wrote it yourself. Will you do that?"

"Yes, sir."

The paper shook as if rattled by wind in the boy's hand. Just as Bob was thinking he should have asked if the boy could read, he saw the smile spread across the tired, young face, and he knew—yes, indeed—the boy was literate.

As if to demonstrate, the boy re-read aloud, "October 30th 1863. To whom it may be of concern to know, Private James B. Jones is hereby discharged and relieved of duty due to a condition of the nerves that renders him unfit for service."

He squinted at an illegible signature before reading, "General, CSA."

He looked at Bob. "Who should I say signed it?"

"Who was your general?"

"Jubal Early."

"Well there you are, then." Bob winked. "That's precisely what I wrote."

As soon as Robbie was down for a nap, Bob assembled his family around the table and took a standing position at the head. His large-knuckled hands held a chair-back, his expression was humorless.

"You all know it's a serious offense to give aid to a Rebel soldier. If anyone in a position of authority asks, you may say we gave food to a discharged private on his way home. There is no reason for details. You may say 'southwestern Virginia' if you must, but I will not name the county of his home. You may say, truthfully, we weren't given a name. You are to say nothing, not one word, to no one unless you are asked, and then only if it is a uniformed soldier. Understood?"

He leaned in Margaret's direction with a hard look. "That includes Rachel Lilly."

Margaret's blond curls bobbed in unison with her head.

"Keep in mind that you would endanger that boy's life by speaking of him, and you would put me at risk of arrest."

Maylene, still recovering from the shock of a loaded rifle pointed at her face, felt her stomach twist with alarm.

Mary spoke first. "I won't say nothing, Papa."

"Nor I," said Melva.

A chorus of agreement echoed around the room.

Sara Mae said, "Now I'm nervous as a cub up a tree."

"Now don't none of you fret. It's unlikely the boy was seen sneaking up or down Madam's Creek, and there's no reason for someone to look here," her husband said. "The Turnpike's where they'll be looking, if any Yankee bothers at all, and I told him he'd best travel at night. When he gets back to Virginia, he's probably in more danger, as a deserter."

"Well, you should have run him off," Sara Mae said.

"Is that what you would have done?" Bob asked, raising his left eyebrow.

Maylene waited for the show of temper that would accompany her mother's defeat.

Sara Mae hesitated, drawing in a long breath between her teeth. "Well, drat you, Robert Nehemiah Farley, you know the answer to that. But that boy had no right to put us at risk."

"He needed help."

"And, Lord knows, he sniffed out the right man!" Sara Mae placed her palms on the table and pushed herself forcefully to her feet, signaling the conclusion of the brief meeting.

That got a laugh from the man who knew his wife could never stay mad at him for more than the time it took for a one-line outburst.

CHAPTER TWELVE

I n early February, a mild spell permitted travel, and Marcus and Corbin were granted furlough, thirty days. Corbin collected Mary and the children and took them down-river to his family's farm. Bob and Sara Mae were alarmed by the prospect of Maylene traveling so close to the end of her pregnancy and asked Marcus to stay there. Maylene thought they were unduly cautious, but Papa responded strongly to her protests.

"Let's think this through. The ride could bring on labor with you this far along. Or you might have the baby when there's deep snow or a bad storm, and your mama can't get up there. It's not wise, Maylene. My answer is no."

Much as she respected her mother-in-law's ability, Maylene had to admit she wanted her mother with her when her time came. She relented, and Marcus accepted the ruling without a word of dissent.

The lack of privacy at the Farley's was agonizing but unavoidable. Margaret and Melva slept in the loft, their parents in a small room—scarcely more than a closet—below. Marcus would have been tempted by the barn if it hadn't been winter.

The couple settled on a straw tick, covered with a woolen rug, in front of the fireplace. There they found it possible to make love, under the sisters, next to the parents, and around Maylene's magnificently bulging belly. Although their setting was far from ideal, they were too overjoyed by their reunion to begrudge it, and they lost much sleep savoring their fleeting hours in each other's company.

Maylene was aware that Marcus was quieter than usual, reserved, but she blamed it on living with his in-laws. It was immediately clear he didn't want to talk about his life as a soldier. So they reminisced, they touched, they talked about baby Quentin, unsure why they both expected a boy.

Marcus rested his head next to Maylene's belly button one night. "I just got kicked. Or maybe punched."

"Serves you right. You're crowding him. He's showing you who's boss."

"Uppity little cuss."

"You'll be a good father."

Marcus kept to himself the mixture of excitement and regret that had come with that news, knowing the words in his answering letter—This extra news is beyond good—were as close as he'd ever come to lying to Maylene. He'd had so little opportunity to explore his role as husband. Now he was to be a father. He didn't feel ready.

He shifted up to eye level. "I'll do my best. It's still hard to imagine. You'll be all right, won't you?"

"I'll be fine." She didn't want to disclose her apprehension to him. He would worry enough without reviewing the dangers.

"You're what keeps me going, you know."

"It's very hard?"

"Not all the time."

"Feel me thinking of you if it helps."

"Sometimes I do feel it. I'll be thinking of something else and there you are. Straight out of the blue. It's like you're right there, and then you're gone again."

"When it's over, we'll not part again."

"We shan't." And he kissed her to seal the promise before turning his attention to the dying fire.

Maylene had already knit wool socks and long, fingerless gloves for Marcus and Johnny. She and Margaret busied themselves weaving flannel and making undershirts. Maylene said the rag Marcus was wearing wasn't fit for wiping mud off a boot.

Marcus pulled on the thick garment the day before his departure and said, "I'm as warm as by the fire."

Maylene said, "That's the heat of my heart sewn in." She took one of his hands, kissed the palm, and pressed it against his chest.

Marcus cleared his throat and reached for his shirt. A rush of shame came on the heels of a flash of anger. He didn't want her to say such things. It was all he could do not to wince at her words, which dropped like iodine into an open wound. He was preparing himself to leave, stepping back into the armor that kept him from missing her madly. She mustn't say and do such things, unforgettable things that could erode his defenses, make mockery of them.

Marcus found Johnny sick when he got back, a bad cold with a cough. Johnny shrugged it off and refused to let Marcus take his picket duty that wet night.

He did put on the new undershirt with a moan of pleasure. "This here will set me right."

The next night, sleet rattled against the hut as Marcus boiled water in a small kettle over the fire. They were out of coffee again, hot water would have to do. Johnny had gotten worse. He couldn't stop shivering.

By midnight the sleet had turned to snow and the wind had strengthened. It was blowing out of the east, never a good sign. Marcus banked the fire and curled up next to Johnny, resigned to the coughing that would keep them and their hut-mates awake.

The next day the storm became a blizzard, and the temperature plummeted. Except for the spells when Johnny threw off his and Marcus's blankets, complaining that he was roasting, Marcus couldn't keep his brother warm. The cough had been joined by a faint wheezing sound. Johnny vomited his breakfast and thereafter refused food.

Making the rounds, Captain Thurmond put his head in. "We'll get him out as soon as we can, son. There's nothing we can do today."

That night, Johnny's fever raged as he exhausted himself forcing air past fluid pooling in his lungs. Marcus replenished the wood supply, boiled more water, said soothing things.

Johnny turned to him with blazing blue eyes. Almost inaudibly he said, "I never told you. I'm happy for you and Maylene. Junior would have come around."

Weary beyond words, Marcus patted his brother's shoulder and nodded his thanks.

Later, while Johnny slept, Marcus ruminated on the words, *Junior would have come around.* It had never once occurred to him that his older brother had coveted his closeness to Maylene. Had he wanted her all along but sensed the futility of trying to come between them? Or had he been too noble to try? With no way to know, Marcus chose the latter explanation before falling into a brief and shallow sleep.

The third day, the storm broke. Two riders were dispatched and returned with news that a couple who had taken in several other sick soldiers that winter was willing to accept another. Johnny toppled when he attempted to stand, then tried to laugh, which triggered a spasm of coughing. The men hoisted him out, his dark, blue-tinged face reminding Marcus of a sky replete with rain. It required a third pair of hands—those of Marcus—to get him onto a saddle, with a rider behind taking the reins.

"See that you stay in the saddle 'til you get where you're going," Marcus chided.

Johnny offered a weak *huzzah* and saluted as the horse stepped out but had to drop his hand to steady himself. His red hair curling out beneath his cap, the only color in the bleached landscape, reminded Marcus of a cardinal on a winter branch. Johnny's fevered breath rose into the cold, still air like a prayer as the pair rode away.

Marcus knew it was too late.

CHAPTER THIRTEEN

Maylene didn't go into labor until the 28th of March. She knew it would be painful but reminded herself women have babies all the time. How awful could it be? Nothing could have prepared her for the hours of contractions, with the added insult of bouts of nausea eased only when an overwhelming desire to push took command. She felt her body had turned on her, inflicting unimaginable suffering.

When she said, "I can't do this no more," Mary said, "If I could do it, you can. You've always been tougher than me."

Sara Mae held her hand. "The baby is coming. It won't be long now. God is watching over you."

Maylene, at that moment, wanted to curse God for making childbirth so wretched, but another contraction made speech impossible.

Yet, suffering as she was, she was not for one moment afraid. As if some natural narcotic entered her brain, she gained a calm assurance she would survive, and her baby, too. If it was a matter of enduring, of completing the ride, she would do it, and she did.

Mama sent Melva to find Papa. Early on, he had saddled Spit in the event that Doc Abshire had to be retrieved from Jumping Branch. Then he spent the day splitting wood and working in the garden like a man possessed, ceaselessly praying.

When darkness fell, he busied himself in the barn. He'd been the same way with Mary, when Sallie Mae was born. His daughters giving birth was the one thing, Sara Mae reckoned, her husband simply couldn't handle.

As Bob hurried in, his wife hurried out. There, on the porch, she let herself cry. She cried because she was so tired. She cried to release the hurt of watching her daughter's hours of painful struggle. And she cried with relief, thanking God Maylene had been safely delivered of her first child. Then she dried her face on a blood-streaked apron hem and returned to the house to start cleaning up and to see if Maylene might have a bit to eat.

The baby was a girl, born with a shocking head of straight black hair. As soon as it was dry, her hair stuck out at all angles, making her look startled. Her eyes were brown, like Marcus's, but a shade darker. She had a broad face and mouth, nothing like her father's and not suggestive of Maylene's either. Maylene couldn't help hoping she would look more like one of her parents as she grew.

The name was a conundrum. Maylene had been sure she was having a boy, a little Marcus. After a few days she settled on Jenny, which sounded much like Johnny, and a little like Quentin. If Marcus didn't like it, they would pick a middle name and call her that.

Jenny was a strong and healthy baby. Her willingness to sleep and her easy nature quickly secured the fondness of mother, aunts, and grandparents. She became their "bundle of joy," passed from the arms of one to another.

Margaret was in particular need of distraction. She had never shown any notable interest in Johnny, until he left home. He had always been "just Johnny." Margaret seemed to be waiting for a better offer to ride up Madam's Creek and whisk her away. His absence, however, had laid bare her attachment to the happy-go-lucky boy she had treated with indifference.

Although Margaret never disclosed the contents of the letter, Maylene suspected some tender words.

Margaret had scarcely eaten for days after news of Johnny's death arrived, but sat silently with downcast, reddened eyes while the family passed dishes of food around her. She held the secret, like a broken wrist tucked in her lap, that she had borrowed money from her grandparents to help Johnny pay for the horse he rode as a Ranger. The horse that enabled him to be with Marcus instead of in the god-awful anonymity of infantry ranks sent east.

Maylene had never seen Margaret in such a state, and it came as a relief to see her sister cuddle Jenny with genuine affection. It was weeks, however, before Margaret was ready to confide.

She came to Maylene, who had recovered sufficiently from childbirth to resume her chores and was hanging laundry. Margaret asked her older sister to walk down to the creek with her. There they sat on a moss-covered log and watched the clear water slip by. Minnows no longer than a willow leaf faced upstream, nearly motionless and invisible in the current. As siblings, no words or eye contact were needed to share closeness. Their silence was a form of communion.

Margaret began.

"I loved him."

"I know you did. When did it start?"

"The day you and Marcus married. Or maybe I always did. I don't know."

Margaret remembered every word of the encounter. Every skin-tingling sensation of it. Johnny had been helping her carry dishes back into the house as the rest of the Farleys said lingering good-byes to the last of their guests. He staggered under what he pretended was a gruesomely heavy load, and made her laugh as he came through the door.

Then he became serious. "Looks like I'll be leaving soon."

"Maylene told me." Unable to meet his gaze, she turned her back to stack dirty plates.

She didn't hear but felt him come close. He was right behind her. She nearly leapt out of her skin when his hand touched her elbow.

"I'm not good at good-byes," he said.

"Nor I." She stood motionless as a corpse.

"Will you turn around?" Now there was the familiar teasing in his voice, and another hand on another elbow.

"If you insist."

She turned and found herself pressed between Johnny and the dry sink. She had never been so close to a boy. An involuntary tremor went through her, to her mortification, but she forced herself to look up, to look Johnny in the eye. It felt too awkward to leave her hands at her sides, so she placed them on his chest. He had regained a gentle grip on her elbows.

His smile was as wide as the sky.

"Can I kiss you good-bye? I might miss you a little."

She gave a nod so faint she wasn't sure if he could detect it. He did.

Johnny moved his right hand to the small of her back, drawing her even closer, and brought his head down, turning his face.... And he planted the softest, sweetest kiss on her lips, the briefest interruption of his blazing smile.

"I'll have another of those for you when I get back," he promised with a wink.

And he left a speechless young Margaret as intoxicated as moonshine would have rendered her. He left her, her heart in full gallop, wondering if she had just been kissed by the boy who would return as the man she would wed.

Margaret dissolved before she could complete her short tale. Maylene, holding and rocking her sister as she sobbed, wished she could cry herself. Her most recent parting from Marcus had been tearless. She had tried to believe she was being brave for his sake, but she knew better. She had become deadened to the pain of separation, as if it were a foul odor she could no longer smell by virtue of its constant presence.

Now, when she ached to put her arms around Marcus and comfort him in the shattering loss of a second brother, she used her sister as a substitute, smoothing her hair and telling her the awful pain wouldn't always feel so sharp.

"You'll be happy again, I promise. Someday happier than you can even imagine."

Maylene did pity her sister, not only for her grief but for the long months she must have awaited with growing despair the letter that never came. She suspected Johnny had been more interested in sewing wild oats than in the long-distance courtship of a girl—then fifteen—who likely felt more like a kid sister than a romantic attraction.

But, owing in part to underestimation of himself, Johnny had greatly underestimated the impact of that first kiss.

Marcus became sullen and withdrawn after Johnny died. Despite lack of evidence to support the notion, he couldn't shake the feeling his brother's death was his fault. Johnny had been his responsibility. He should have protected him better, taken his picket duty, physically forced him to stay in that rainy night if that's what was required. Although by what method he could have coerced his larger brother he didn't know.

It didn't matter. He was supposed to keep his brother alive. He'd been wallowing in the warmth of wife and fireplace while Johnny had been left in that frigid, filthy camp with no one looking out for him. Marcus found no relief in telling himself again and again there was nothing he could have done. The illness, the bitter cold, the storm—all beyond his control. It was God's doing, God's will.

"The Lord giveth and the Lord taketh away." He could hear Pastor Mullens.

The Lord taketh too much, he thought.

Awful as it had been to lose Junior, it was harder to lose Johnny. Junior was intense and competitive, the brother who never failed to beat him in a foot race, a wrestling match, a war of words. He could be harsh with a put-down and short of temper. Despite his physical resemblance to Junior, Johnny was nearly the opposite, quick to joke and make light of even the worst situations. Quick to make friends, quick to forgive. Happy. Marcus felt sure Johnny had forfeited a share of their contests for the sake of an older brother's pride.

Marcus floundered. He struggled to pray for Maylene and his family, feeling his words dropped into a void. How many millions of prayers had gone unanswered since the start of the war? Who was listening?

He stopped praying for himself. He avoided everyone.

Without Johnny, Marcus felt adrift, suspended in a no-man's land of fragile and divided loyalties. As a member of Thurmond's Partisan Rangers, he knew the inevitable brotherhood of men who shared drills, meals, triumphs, dangers, defeats, homesickness, illness and injury, music-making, gags, and every possible trial of living out-of-doors. Despite how he felt about the war and conscription, he had forged bonds with some good-hearted, quirky, and comical men. Those bonds put him at risk, however, of taking risks, and of suffering additional grief.

He fought for the South, but did he want the South to win? He didn't know anymore. Which brother's death was to be for a lost cause? Marcus saw the Yankees as a threat and wanted them gone, but if the South won, slavery would continue. The nation would be split in two, possibly forever. That outcome might encourage other such rebellions in the future. He didn't want his children or theirs to live with that threat. The one thing he knew with certainty about the conflict was that he wanted it to end.

Marcus was loyal to his home and family, but both were increasingly indistinct as time wore on. "Home" was now Union turf, which made it seem a conquered land, more subject to the long arm of federal government. Or was it more independent, having shaken free of "Old Virginia?" Although he was sure he loved them, his parents felt almost like strangers. He could no longer recall the voice of each sibling. Nor could he imagine changes in habit, face, and shape as maturation left its mark. Even Rachel, the sister who had followed him on so many of his expeditions, was losing form, like a reflection in water that slips away when a cloud blocks the sun.

There remained only Maylene, whose warm nakedness within the circle of his arms he could still summon, to hitch his heart to. But loving her meant missing her and fearing for her safety, so even that refuge carried cost.

Vaguely, Marcus knew he was spiraling into himself with no clear return path. The trouble was, he didn't care.

Mr. Bennett sought him out one spring evening, soon after the Rangers had abandoned their winter camp and taken up their roaming life again. Jefferson Bennett, approaching his mid-fifties, was a father of eight who had enlisted—much to the displeasure of his wife—soon after the war began. Marcus knew him as the outspoken farmer who harangued anyone who would listen, up at Meador's Store, about the evil ways of Lincoln and northern Republicans. He had a knack for riling people up, long before the first shots of war were fired.

"Son, I know you're broke up about losing your brother. But keep in mind how proud we are of him. He may not have died in battle, but in his short time with us he did more for the morale of this company than anyone else. Mark my words, he kept men from quarrelling, from deserting, and from wallowing in self-pity. You must honor him and carry on in a manner worthy of him."

Marcus, astride a felled dead hickory, kept his eyes on the stout stick he whittled as anger rose like a bad aftertaste in his throat. He wanted to say, For what? So I can die, too, for something I never wanted no part of?

The last thing he wanted was a pep talk from Mr. Bennett. But he also didn't want to offend the man who was attempting a fatherly role, as he often did with his "boys," one of which was his eldest son, Robert.

"I'll keep that in mind."

"See that you do, Lilly. You're a fine soldier, too, and you'll make your pa as proud as my Robert makes me."

Mr. Bennett gave Marcus a couple of confirming whacks on his right shoulder, and it was all Marcus could do not to haul off and slug him.

He continued carving. Onto the blunt ends of cherry or chestnut limbs, he whittled the shapes of his childhood fantasies—the head of a horse, a turtle, a raven. He carved a snake, a frog. He carved the Hooded Thief with an X in place of one eye. As he completed each one, he tossed it into the cook-fire and began a new one. The stories escaped him now, but it soothed him to use his hands.

The spring of 1864 was not to be a normal one, not that anything had been normal since the declaration of war. There was an especially late freeze, which devastated the Farleys' garden. Cabbage, turnips, onions, carrots, and beets were relatively unfazed, but the rest browned and curled as if poisoned with salt. Maylene couldn't bear to see their efforts turned to rot—young greens of tomatoes, squash, beans, cucumbers, potatoes, corn…. Although the pea plants withstood the freeze, their blossoms did not, putting an early end to much of the crop.

There was nothing to do but start over. Bob Farley was a cautious man, who always reserved seed for such an occasion. There wasn't as much as there had been for the first round, but the garden was replanted, getting a weeks-late start on the growing season. The entire family was relieved to see new sprouts thrusting out of the dark alluvial soil by the second week of June.

About the time the garden was coming back to life, there was a day of steady rain. That night, Maylene woke to approaching thunder, a continuous percussion. Flashes of light grew brighter as the storm neared, illuminating the beams above her in the small room she shared with her sisters. Jenny, in her cradle at the base of the bed, was a sound sleeper, thankfully. Only the loudest of thunderclaps was likely to disturb her.

Maylene heard the shushing sound of rain hitting leaves before it began to pelt the cabin roof. Heavy rain, torrential. She lay awake waiting for it to lessen but soon drifted off.

She awoke again in faint light. Jenny was crying to be fed. It was still raining, hard, and a new sound had joined that of the rain. It was a sound she knew, the creek was up. Maylene rose and went to the small loft window. She could make out a swath of water, three or four times wider than normal, swirling downstream. Madam's Creek had jumped its banks.

Papa was up. She heard him putting on boots by the door and thought how reassuring it was to have him there. His presence was her one benefit of living in a Union state. Had West Virginia not succeeded in its bid for statehood, Papa would have been drafted by now. Her father, a grandfather. The Confederacy had once again expanded the age range for conscription: seventeen to fifty.

Nevertheless, Maylene felt uneasy as she nursed Jenny at the kitchen table, waiting for the chicory-root coffee her mother prepared. High water was nothing new, but it was unusual at this time of year.

Switching Jenny to the other breast, Maylene looked up. Thunder sounded ominously from the west again. By the time she finished her coffee and moved her baby to burping position, the rain had re-intensified to downpour.

Three hours later, there was no sign of letup, and the creek had run amuck. It was frothing, brown, carrying fence rails and whole trees, whose roots projected upward like the hands of drowning men seeking a handhold. The lower edge of the garden had gone under. Part of the cornfield was awash. Papa released the chickens, knowing they would move to higher ground. With help from Melva and Margaret, and with Robbie yelling on the sidelines, he chased the pig out of its sty to join the sheep, cow, and mules, safe on their sloping pasture.

The creek kept rising.

With sinking stomachs, the family watched their bridge go under, knowing it couldn't possibly survive the onslaught. Round after round of storm swept across the sky, as if pinpointing their very farm.

The cabin was safe, positioned well above the narrow floodplain. Water began to lap at the barn, however, for the first time in its existence, and by the end of the day—despite a lessening of rainfall—the fields of corn and wheat were entirely submerged. Much of the hayfield had gone under. The garden, its location no longer discernable, had drowned.

Bob paced back and forth on the porch, checking the sky, watching with growing despair for flotsam to appear at the water's edge, signaling retreat.

Sara Mae called out to him, "You might as well come in and eat. It don't do you no good looking at that sorry mess."

Bob grunted before answering. "I'll be in in a bit. You all go on and eat."

Sara Mae sat down with emphasis. "Let him go hungry if that's what he wants. I don't see no point in starving before we have to. He's worse than a cow a'grievin' over a dead calf."

Maylene empathized with her father. It was all she could do to force down the meal of beans, spring onions, salted pork, and buttermilk. Sensitive to the tension around the table, even

Jenny was fussy. Maylene soothed her by letting her nurse. There was no comfort for the rest of the family, however, dining wordlessly to the soft drone of rain on the roof.

Just before dark, the rain drizzled to a stop. An hour later, Bob stood forlornly at the upper edge of the garden, holding a beeswax-burning lamp, when he saw the collecting spittle of bark bits, twigs, sawdust and leaf fragments that satisfied him the water was dropping. He returned to the cabin with slow steps, dreading what the morning would reveal.

It was pretty much as he'd pictured it. The garden was a lost cause. The corn and wheat fields were largely buried in silt. Even the hayfield was damaged, with shallow gullies and wide, sinuous sandbars where there should have been lush grass. Boot-sucking mud extended many yards from the still-raging water, and closer to the creek was a great tangle of whole trees, partial trees, branches of trees. Debris already dangled above Bob's head, where descending water had discarded it in standing box-elders and sycamores.

Bob sat down on a muddy log and tugged his lower lip. He didn't know where to start.

That question was answered in the afternoon, when it became evident the bridge was gone. The farm was now bisected, with no way across the stream's steep banks to the Madam's Creek road. Not that the road was in any shape to be of much use at present.

Once set in motion, Bob Farley was a man of single-minded focus. He had Dolly and Spit in harness before sunrise the next day. As soon as a hasty breakfast of eggs, fatback, and cornbread was cleared, he headed upslope with stout rope, a two-man saw, an axe, and log tongs, intent on cutting timbers for a new bridge. He took with him two assistant lumberjacks, his wife and second daughter.

CHAPTER FOURTEEN

Quentin Lilly's stint in the Army was relatively brief, which was a blessing in more ways than one. He was a proud man, unused to taking orders, and certainly not from men half his age. He was reprimanded more than once for a certain tardiness and resentment that accompanied his consent to be commanded. Quentin feared it was only a matter of time before he snapped and wound up severely disciplined. Yet he was respected for his steadiness and stoicism in battle, which calmed the younger men. Even his bearlike shape—wide and long on torso, short and thick on legs—was reassuring. He seemed immovable and indestructible as a pasture boulder.

In May of 1864, at Virginia's Cloyd's Mountain, the rock proved mortal. Quentin was sent on horseback to relay a message when the horse was shot out from under him at a full gallop. His right leg was broken, the knee twisted and crushed. The tibia would heal, but the outrageously swollen knee looked doubtful.

The field surgeon said, "You've got no words I haven't heard," as he squeezed, prodded, and flexed the knee to the accompaniment of every profane expletive Quentin knew.

His inspection completed, he said, "The kneecap is in pieces. There's ligaments torn. That knee is ruined beyond hope of repair."

And Quentin soon received an order he executed with enthusiasm: Discharged, go home.

He arrived to find the garden in shambles. Suzanne, with a wish and a prayer, had planted virtually every seed. There remained a dozen tomato seeds and a few handfuls of beans to replant after the late freeze. Weeds grew where there should have been orderly rows of green. Quentin stood propped on a homemade crutch, calculating the loss, shaking his head.

His daughters began hoeing and yanking weeds at once, if only to make the garden look less distressing. Some of the strawberries were growing back, they reported.

Suzanne and Eliza mothered Quentin until he bellowed, "I may be a crippled man, but I'm still a man. Let me do for myself!"

At their begging for tales of warfare, he told Calvin and Lester they were too young. "Ask me again in five years," he said, adding under his breath, "With luck, I'll have forgotten it all by then."

Their pleas were not easily subdued, however. To mollify them, Quentin used his crutch as a rifle, resting it on the porch railing.

"See yonder, coming down through the woods?"

"Where?" Lester asked, his hazel eyes wide.

Quentin noticed Lester's riotous, dark-blond hair had nearly reached those eyes. "Son, you need a haircut."

Quentin turned his attention back to the woods above the pasture and squinted, taking aim. "Hush! There's Yankees coming. Git down!"

The boys crouched.

"Easy now," Quentin whispered. "They ain't spotted us yet. You boys sneak around behind the barn and wheat field, and head up through the woods. Circle 'round and take 'em by surprise from behind."

"We got no guns!" Calvin pointed out.

"No, but you're quicker than they are, and when you yell, you'll scare the bejesus out of them. Put some stones in your pockets in case any of 'em don't run off real quick. I'll cover you from here and give those fellers a warm reception."

The boys ran toward the barn, half-believing there were enemy soldiers behind every tree. Minutes later, Quentin laughed at their screams as they drove the bluecoats from the hillside. But no sooner had his amusement subsided than a shroud of sadness descended upon him, attended by a thirst for whiskey.

From that time forward, Calvin and Lester needed no prompting to chase Yankees of their own invention, and their pa was content to stay out of the game.

Beyond his resistance to pampering, Quentin made no complaint, despite pain with every unsteady step. He had seen enough suffering to feel he'd been fortunate. He was alive and home, and he thanked God, but he couldn't help feeling shame about being safe while Marcus remained in the fray. It didn't sit right. He prayed for his son to join him before another winter in the field.

Resting on the porch with Suzanne that summer, Quentin looked out at the farm he loved. Far larger than the Farley farm, it was a portrait of both benevolence and harshness. Much of the corn had survived the freeze. The wheat and hay thrived. The pastures rolled upward, vivid green with the exception of stumps and stones. Yet, with two sons dead and one away, with one leg useless, with Calvin and Lester too small to be of much help, Quentin considered how the weight of labor rested on the backs of his wife and four daughters. They deserved better. The war had turned everything upside down. Women wrestled plows across the stony earth. Men cried like infants. Families, their homes burned to the ground, were forced to live in caves. It seemed the very fabric of life had been bunched by a malevolent hand that refused to let go. He longed for it to lie smooth again.

CHAPTER FIFTEEN

The bullet that found Marcus did so indirectly. He and three others had been sent to high ground—a rock-strewn rise with scattered cedars—to provide cover for the raid of a supply train. Marcus crouched behind a limestone boulder, his rifle barrel resting on its rounded surface, watching the stealthy movements of the men below as they prepared an ambush along the road running north out of Union. A cicada droned in the distance, making him feel sluggish in the heat and harsh late-morning light. The grumbling of his empty stomach was too familiar to be distracting, but Marcus reminded himself to ignore his thirst and desire for shade, to remain alert and focused on his task of vigilance.

There was no longer a soldier in sight. All had vanished, along with their horses, into heavy woods on the east side of the road. Marcus was shifting his weight slightly when he heard a shot. At the same instant, something materialized from his shielding rock and slammed into his face. He felt a giant fist—a fist with a knife in it—had struck him in his right eye. Stunned and bleeding, he fell to his knees, dropping his rifle. Immediately he groped for his weapon, but his vision was blurred in one eye, non-existent in the other. The ground was playing tricks on him, tilting and pivoting. Feeling exposed, he flattened himself on the unsteady earth, aware of small stones poking his ribs and thighs. He pulled his pistol out its holster—his right boot—and tried again to focus, unsure where to direct his tear-smeared gaze.

Within seconds, Corbin was there. Before Marcus grasped what was happening, Corbin unsheathed his knife, clamped Marcus's head between his elbow and thigh, and cut free the dangling, ruined eyeball with the matter-of-factness of a farmer castrating a calf. Lacking anything better, he yanked off his wool cap and told Marcus to press it against the wound. Steady Corbin. He kept talking, saying they had returned fire and driven the sniper away, explaining what was going on below as the failed attack turned into retreat, complaining about a lost button of all things. He kept talking in a low, even tone, and Marcus held onto that stream of words like a rope as he lay on the ground, swimming through pain and nausea, held afloat by the sound of Corbin's voice.

The bullet had fractured the rock's crown, sending a dagger of it directly into the eye socket. The wound wept and oozed for weeks, yet it somehow healed under a crusty patch.

Spectacular discoloration surrounding the eye socket, which the patch was unable to mask, prompted Jeff Bennett to say, "Boy, you look like you wrassled the Devil himself and came out on the losing end."

Marcus was left with a badly scarred upper eyelid, fused to the less-damaged lower lid. The biggest change, once the pain and swelling subsided, was his lost marksmanship. It wasn't evident until his attempt to wing a Federal soldier went wrong.

Late that summer, a small contingent of blue-coated scouts was spotted watering their horses in Monroe County's Indian Creek alongside a supply route the Thurmond Rangers guarded. A party of snipers was put in motion without delay.

A fleeting grimace crossed Marcus's face. As a member of the select force, he understood why he'd been chosen to be part of this distasteful duty.

The Rangers, having correctly guessed the timing and route of the scouting party, lay in wait within a small log barn. They had knocked out enough chinking to make room for gun barrels and felt cockily secure, their horses likewise out of sight within the cramped and stifling space.

Corporal Warren raised his right arm as the Union men approached, their horses raising minor explosions of dust with each stride. "Steady now. Aim for the man in the order in which we stand."

Marcus felt the familiar gathering of dread—his pulse picked up speed, his mouth went dry, and his armpits began drenching his already-sweat-dampened wool uniform. He zeroed in on his target, a short-looking man on a gray mount, a soldier with a mustache but no beard. As the group of fifteen came closer, Marcus squinted at the precise spot—his victim's right shoulder. He would be damned if he'd shoot a man in the chest in cold blood. A man with no chance to defend himself. It wasn't right. Even aiming for a shoulder from his position of safety felt cowardly.

Warren snatched his own rifle stock. In a hushed tone, he gave the deadly order, "Ready.... Aim..."

A young recruit had been given the task of distracting the horses with a can of oats, but he didn't have their pecking order sorted out. A loud squeal of dominance from a mare made the men jump.

The Union horses and their riders turned to look at the barn. "Fire!"

The barn shook with sound and filled instantly with smoke. After firing, Marcus remained motionless, watching his man recoil, clutch at his upper chest with one hand, pull his pistol from its holster with the other, and slump across his prancing horse's neck. Was he vomiting? No, it was blood coming from his mouth.

Sweet Jesus, I've done hit his lung.

Marcus cried out. It was hardly the triumphant shout of his comrades.

Did I truly expect to escape the war without killing a man? Marcus reloaded with awkward hands, spilling powder.

He hung back when the others galloped forward to chase survivors and inspect casualties. "Inspection of casualties" amounted to wholesale theft. Not only weapons and items of clothing were taken but such personal effects as money, combs, and pens. It was not unusual for men too badly wounded to be taken prisoner to be left behind with the dead, stripped down to their shirts and drawers or pantaloons.

Ashamed of his inability to approach the injured and dying men—one in particular—Marcus mounted Blackjack and busied himself collecting several riderless horses, which had galloped up the road a short distance with the spooked Union survivors, and then sensibly stopped to graze.

The Rangers regrouped and made a hasty getaway, eager to be on the move before the departing Federals realized they outnumbered the men who had ambushed them, or, worse, had a chance to alert reinforcements.

Desperate to avoid a repeat mistake, Marcus overcame his reticence enough to seek out Captain Thurmond the next day. "Sir, it became evident yesterday my aim is off."

Will he change my duties?

The captain leaned back in a folding field chair, stroked his dark beard. "Private Lilly, you may not be the marksman you once were, but you remain of value to us. If you're fishing for a discharge, you'll not have it."

Marcus felt slapped. Color rose in his cheeks. "It's not that, sir. I wanted you to know."

"You may consider me informed."

"Yes, sir."

Able to think of nothing further to say, Marcus saluted and turned on his heels. It was to be the last time he spoke to the Captain.

That September, at Tazewell, Virginia, the company joined forces with Witcher's cavalry battalion, their goal being a coordinated attack on Union outposts in West Virginia. They enjoyed a string of successes, including a raid on Bulltown, where they burned a Union fort, and another raid on Weston, where they confiscated supplies and lifted over five thousand dollars from the Weston Exchange Bank. Next, at Buckhannon, they captured a Union garrison. By the time they circled south to Greenbrier County, they had amassed several hundred horses and cattle, as well as approximately three hundred prisoners of war.

"Thou shalt not steal."

Marcus had given up his scruples in that regard. The Rangers were sorely in need of food and the most basic of supplies, which the Confederacy found increasingly difficult to provide. Part of their motivation was staying alive.

By mid-October, the combined cavalries were camped in southwestern West Virginia when they received a scouting report that Union forces had occupied Winfield on the Kanawha River. An unacceptable taking. Winfield must be reclaimed.

Late that month, the Confederates arrived under cover of darkness. Marcus was near the rear of his column, which followed a small stream into town. The startled Union pickets were driven in, allowing the Rangers to surround the Union quarters. Without waiting for the second column, Captain Philip Thurmond launched a charge, taking the lead position. He was felled as soon as Union troops opened fire. Marcus had just slipped out of formation and into the night's oblivion when he was passed by the captain being hurriedly carried to the rear, a soldier's hands pressed on an abdominal wound. Soon forced to retreat, the Rangers left Thurmond in the care of his younger brother, Elias, who allowed himself to be captured and remained at Philip's side until his death, which came on winged feet. The unsuccessful engagement lasted no more than an hour. The demoralized Confederate contingent then evaporated into the dark—evading pursuit by a much smaller Union force—taking with it eighteen stolen horses.

Even in the absence of war, horse stealing was an efficient way to get oneself killed. Nevertheless, Marcus had long since won the title, Horse-Thief-in-Chief. His ability to move silently enabled him to slip into paddocks undetected or release horses tied to trees without disturbing them. He had a way with animals, they trusted him. He would sometimes carry a stale morsel of cornbread or a handful of oats in his pocket, with which he could identify the dominant horse. Once that horse was led away, the others would follow.

The eighteen horses taken that night at Winfield were largely his doing.

Losing an eye helped Marcus. He was able to shed some of the insidious guilt he felt about Johnny. With two brothers dead, Marcus carried a subconscious conviction he shouldn't escape unscathed. The war ought to mark him in a permanent way, allowing him to wear his grief in physical form.

"Eye for eye, tooth for tooth." There was that, too, the sense that retribution was owed for the harm he'd inflicted.

The injury, once fully healed, began pulling Marcus out of his despondency. It reminded him that he wanted to live. Had it been the bullet, not the rock fragment, that had taken his eye, he would most certainly be dead. He might well find meaning in that, express a measure of gratitude.

He began to take interest in the newer recruits, who kept getting more youthful-looking. Volunteers in their early teens—and even younger—were being welcomed into the ranks of the Confederacy, even if only to serve as drummers, barbers, and water carriers. To Marcus, the adolescents' strutting bravado was a feeble attempt to mask homesickness and anxiety. He left military training to the officers but instructed the lads in basic aspects of staying alive—how to avoid dehydration, frostbite, and heat exhaustion. He taught them how to spare their horses unnecessary strain and be alert for signs of lameness. He was a natural teacher, having had much practice with seven younger siblings, and the green privates took to him as a trusted big brother.

In quiet moments, Marcus repeated to himself he was a father. In a cabin on Madam's Creek waited an infant boy or girl with his name or face or capacity for imagining. A baby who needed a pa. He was determined to return home as he'd promised and lie tangled with Maylene in the same sublime exhaustion of their honeymoon week, the week he returned to again and again when he was most in need of inspiration.

By the time the last leaves dropped that fall, Marcus Lilly had shaken off the remaining tendrils of depression. He faced forward, resolutely determined to live.

CHAPTER SIXTEEN

Unable to put up enough food, the Farleys faced a hard winter. Short on both hay and corn, Bob was forced to do something he'd never done before, slaughter a healthy dairy cow. A frenzy of meat preservation followed, salting and pickling and smoking. Nothing would be wasted.

Bob then took a job re-roofing a house and preparing firewood for a widow on Ellison Ridge. After nearly two weeks of work, he took the wagon up to collect his payment, a pair of dairy goats. With their ability to forage on almost anything, he was confident of keeping them fed, even if it meant cutting brush along the creek.

With any luck, the hens would lay well into the winter. The goats would provide milk, and the bees, bothered by neither chill nor flood, had made much honey. The apples had set fruit before the catastrophic freeze. Survivors of burial in mud, there were beets and carrots, too, in the apple house. Onions. Turnips. Thanks to the cow, ample beef. The family would soon partake of the annual ritual of hog slaughter. Chestnuts, walnuts, butternuts, and dried mushrooms were stockpiled. Bob would hunt mallards in the shallows along the river edge until ice drove them to deeper water. The Farleys would not starve.

But they would miss the mainstay of their diet, corn. Without it, no corn pone, no johnnycakes, no spoon bread, and no grits. Also missing were jar upon jar of canned vegetables that would normally line their shelves. And two goats did not equal one cow—there would be far less milk, cream, and butter. Wheat flour, since the start of the war, was nearly nonexistent. Its shortage was a moot point, however, as the family lacked cash to purchase it.

Bob took his hunting partners, Mary and Melva, in search of a buck. They returned with a squirrel and a crow.

It wasn't like being a soldier, Maylene reminded herself. The family's hardships that winter couldn't be compared with those of the men out there in the field with their makeshift housing, inadequate clothing, and frozen toes. Yet it was impossible not to watch with alarm as their stores of food dwindled. By December the hens had stopped laying. Excess roosters having already been consumed, the Farleys feasted on roasted and fried hens until the flock was shrunk to winter size.

Chicken-culling completed, food gaps became more glaring. Missed as much as cornmeal were beans—both pickled and dried—and potatoes. Although some replanted potato plants had come gasping out of the muck, most had suffocated. More than anything, Maylene knew she'd hunger for her favorite winter staple, Sara Mae's potato chowder, seasoned with onions and ham. Soon after Christmas, the last potful was served like a sacrament.

The next day, Bob hitched up the mule team to deliver Mary and her children to the Radcliff farm. Better to swallow his pride than watch them go hungry.

Shortly after setting out and sensing her father's discomfort, Mary commented that Robbie would benefit from playing with a Radcliff cousin close to his age.

"I suppose he will," her papa said without turning his head.

Mary added, "We'll be back in a few months, and Robbie will help you plant, won't you, sweetie? You know how to put the seeds in the ground. Remember last spring?"

Seated between his mother and grandfather, Robbie shrugged and flipped the end of a check line back and forth. "I'd rather dig taters."

"Well that's later, in the fall. You have to plant before you can dig."

"Bah, humbug," answered three-and-a half-year-old Robbie. He'd recently learned the expression from Melva and used it often. But he, too, looked straight ahead and missed his mama's smile.

So Mary did what she'd learned from her mama to do when someone needs cheering up—she sang. Softly, she began with one of Papa's favorites. "As I gaed o'er the Highland hills, to a farmer's house I came; the night being dark and something wet I ventured into the same, where I was kindly treated, and a pretty girl I spied, who asked me if I had a wife? But marriage I denied."

Neither Papa nor Robbie joined in. Two-year-old Sallie Mae, however, beamed and inserted words from her seat on Mary's lap until the ballad concluded with the rejection of the pretty girl—"Although we at a distance are, and the seas between us roar, yet I'll be constant, Peggy Bawn, to thee for ever more."

Undaunted, Mary tried another known favorite. "One night upon my rambles, two miles above Fermoy, I met a farmer's daughter, all on the mountains high," she sang, louder this time.

But by the time she reached the final line with a hearty "sly, bold Reynardine," she was beginning to despair. When had she ever seen her pa so crestfallen? Not since... no, she wasn't going to revisit that March when she was in the seventh grade and thought she'd never see her papa smile again.

Surely he felt embarrassment, even shame, to unload three of his dependents on another family, but it wasn't as if it was his fault the Farleys had too little food.

Mary thought of another song, her last hope. This day she would sing it and not cry. "Gaily the troubadour touched his guitar when he was hast'ning home from the war...."

And Robbie, knowing what came next, chimed in. "Singing from Palestine, hither I come; lady love, lady love, welcome me home."

Bob Farley felt as beaten as an old rug, but his daughter had landed on the one ballad he could not refuse. The mules rocked back their long, velvety ears to take in his voice, "…hither I come; lady love, lady love, welcome me home."

The trio sang "Gaily the Troubadour" three times. By then Sallie Mae was fast asleep. Framing pink cheeks, her brown hair curled out from her gray woolen bonnet. Her arms hung limp as a ragdoll's. She didn't hear her brother ask what a troubadour is or see that her grandpa was a fair bit more himself.

The new year, 1865, began with biting cold. There wasn't a night Maylene didn't go to bed with a hollow stomach, or a morning she didn't wake up ravenous. Still, her body produced milk, and Jenny continued to grow. At her mother's expense. Maylene lost weight faster than the others.

The family stopped attending church, instinctively recognizing the need to stay close to the fire, conserve energy. Mama would read from the Bible on Sunday mornings, and they would pray and sing. Always, Papa reminded them to be grateful for what they had, that things could be worse. There were those who'd had their homes burned, food stolen, horses taken.

"We must remember," Papa said, "what others endure."

As the hay supply dwindled, Melva and Margaret were given the task of taking the mules outside the pasture to graze. They would tie a disgruntled Spit to a tree and leave Dolly feeding on grass near the road or creek, then switch the captive mule a few hours later. Securing one mule was equivalent to securing both, because neither would stray far from the other.

By late January, a deep melancholy had settled over Maylene and she stopped counting the days until spring. Winter's end felt impossibly far away, as did Marcus's return. She scolded herself. Here she was, months from the long awaited reunion, and she could no longer hold the image before her. It slipped from her focus like fog parting before the lamp when Papa left the house to milk the goats. She wanted only to sleep like a hibernating bear, curl and sleep until she could feel like being alive again.

She tried to resurrect the fantasy life of her girlhood. She dredged her memory for Marcus's fanciful tales. She unearthed nothing but fragments and found herself unable to maintain coherent thought long enough to weave a story that would take her out of the cramped cabin with its shrinking food supply.

She looked at her chapped hands, red and cracked from washing woven squares of flannel that served as diapers. Endless piles of diapers that must be washed in a pot of hot water over the fire, then hung, dripping—whenever it was too dark, too cold, or too wet to hang them outside—on a string Papa had hung from wall to wall. Pot after pot of soiled water was dumped off the porch. How could one baby possibly produce so much mess? How could Mary have gone through this twice and had any skin left on her hands?

Maylene sought out her pa. Mama would be sympathetic but was likely to offer prayer and Scripture as remedies, and Maylene had worn those options to the bone. Papa would listen more, talk less—there was something comforting in that, something she needed.

She found him by the barn on a blustery winter afternoon, his back to her, preparing Spit to move a load of seasoned firewood from barn to porch. His chilled hands were awkward, and he dropped the harness before getting it in place across Spit's dark back. With seeming innocence, Spit put a near front hoof on a strap just as Papa's hand reached down for the harness.

"Git off it!" Bob snapped, still doubled over and leaning a shoulder roughly against Spit's. Instead of stepping away, Spit leaned right back.

Maylene folded her arms across her chest, prepared to be amused. For years she had taken mischievous pleasure in the love-hate relationship that existed between her father and the male mule. They had developed a grudging respect for each other, and even flirted with genuine affection. Then, on the cusp of friendship, Spit would inevitably assert his right to mulishness, and Papa would scorn the day he bought the unpromising colt. But Bob Farley had a rare patience with both his children and his animals. Negotiations would begin once more for the tenuous truce that allowed man and mule to function as a team.

Maylene expected to see her father's mock indignation, followed by the firm and persistent persuasion—without a trace of harshness—that would bring Spit into line.

She stood up straighter when her father yelled, "Useless, cussed beast—move!"

This sounded like real anger.

Bob was upright now, and he placed both hands on Spit's muscular shoulder. He shoved. Spit leaned toward him again and swung his head around for an attempted bite. Maylene watched her father leap like a flushed cottontail—dodging the bite—ball up a fist, and hit Spit's shoulder with all he had.

Spit grunted, flipped his tail in disgust, and stepped off the harness. His ears-laid-back glare said volumes about what he'd like to do to one Robert Farley.

Maylene felt shock and shame, as if she had witnessed an indecency. A fit of temper, coming from her father, felt like a hole torn in the sky. It was impossible. As her father tightened straps with jerking motions, she turned and hastened away. She did not want to see his face.

It was Mama who came to the rescue. She placed a bag of duck-down and several old flour sacks next to the fire. "We are going to make a comforter for you and Marcus," she said.

Maylene numbly obeyed, working whenever Jenny napped or was occupied with a kindly aunt, as the motion of her hands sent a current of warmth farther and farther up her arms and into her body, reaching at last her core. She began to awaken and shake off her lethargy, joining her mother singing hymns and Irish ballads as their fingers made tiny stitches in the coarse cloth.

Lured by their voices, Papa sat himself down, fixed his eyes on the darting flames, and harmonized in a baritone as rich and warm as fresh cream. As snow swirled in small eddies off the roof, their music rose above their winter-thinned forms and into the night sky, smeared with the Milky Way's parade of stars. There, deep in the mountains, in a land beaten down by nearly four years of civil war and every imaginable horror it could offer, beauty remained. Madam's Creek murmured toward the New, like a promise nature's course, akin to that of the human heart, would follow an instinctive path homeward.

March pushed the last of the ice down the New, melting as it went. Its passage reminded Maylene of an anniversary, and she took the path to the little plot where Robin and her grandparents rested. There wasn't much to the grave-site, an overgrown clearing the size of a bedroom.

Maylene's Farley grandparents had been infertile, or so they thought, until baby Robert took them by surprise when they were closing in on forty. What they'd lacked in children, they had made up for in optimism. The sturdy mountain wagon—a luxury known to none of their neighbors—was one of the fruits of that forward-looking confidence in a future that was sure to bring better roads and bigger crops. Maylene's grandpa had built the wagon himself.

Maylene always thought her papa's parents must have worked themselves to death on their little farm. They died before she was born and were laid side by side where their souls could look down on the farm, the creek, and a short stretch of river. Well, in winter they could, before the leaves came out.

Maylene read the names, Mary S. Farley and Graham R. Farley. They'd died within a year of one another.

Where, Maylene wondered for the first time, is Papa's first wife buried? Why isn't she here?

She'd never given her any real thought, as if Papa's life had begun with her first memories.

Something clicked. Surely Papa's first wife had died in childbirth, and that was why Papa had been such a wreck when Sallie and Jenny were born right here on the farm, under his roof.

Oh, Papa.

A vigorous wind gave voice to treetops far above but only stirred dry leaves around Maylene, pocketed as she was within the steep-walled valley cut over the eons by the creek below. Warmed from the ascent, she gathered her skirts about her legs and sat next to her brother's grave. The wind sounded mournful and pushed her thoughts into the shadowy recesses she preferred to avoid.

She imagined cigar-smoking men in distant places, Washington and Richmond, making puff-chested decisions that wreaked havoc all the way to the remotest outposts. How could their bony fingers reach so far that they ferreted out Marcus and Johnny, tucked in this sheltered fold—one of countless like it in the rumpled sprawl of Appalachia? Did they have any idea of the depth and breadth of suffering their posturing spawned?

It wasn't that pre-war life had been a picnic, free of toil and sadness. The mountains provided, but the stony soil wasn't easily farmed, and the higher spots held graves of the many Robins laid to rest. And yet. Life followed predictable patterns, as reliable as the flow of water downstream, held upright by three pillars—faith in one another, faith in the land, and faith in God.

Maylene could feel that three-legged stool giving way beneath her as the Union-Confederacy divide continued to drive a wedge into the heartwood of community. People locked doors, spoke in whispers, distrusted strangers, and stayed close to home. Who could you trust entirely but your own family? Even there, treachery was not unknown.

In recent months it had become clear the Confederacy was losing ground. Had God turned His back on the South? So many women in black, so many fatherless children. Disfigured survivors. Abject poverty. Fear of what was to come. Were these all their stalwart faith had wrought? Maylene's prayers had been repeated enough to become a mantra, their meaning lost in a hum of syllables as undirected as floating leaves.

Maylene had always felt held in the caring hand of her hollow. Mountains rising on three sides had felt protective, like the wings of a hen over her chicks. Her foundation had been shaken by the freeze and flood that had ravaged the farm—even the land seemed intent on retribution.

But Maylene's connection to the earth went deep as a hickory taproot. The flood had brought nutrients in the mire it left behind. The yields of fields and garden were likely to be especially high this year. And the wild foods remained, signs of God's abundance. There had been gifts, too, from neighbors. No one had anything to spare, yet a slab of bacon, a half dozen sweet potatoes, a crock of elderberry jam—these and other items had been slipped into her parents' hands after church on a number of Sundays.

In addition, traditions of shared labor endured. Families came together to shuck out a cornfield, construct a new fence, erect a cabin, grub a field free of stumps, or scutch flax in preparation for spinning into linen. For generations, pioneers had survived by helping one another, and Maylene knew those who retreated from that heritage did so at their peril.

She wasn't ready to lose all faith. She would press on. Everything would be easier if Marcus were sitting here beside her, commenting on the nuthatch inching down a nearby sugar-maple trunk.

She was starting to get cold. Maylene ran her hand along the top of Robin's stone, remembering his ready laughter, his piping voice. She recalled holding him on her lap and kissing his hair the color and softness of milkweed down. His death had left her afraid. If she died, would Papa never speak of her again, never visit her grave?

If Marcus died, she would speak of him the rest of her life.

She pressed her forehead against her knees, willing the panic away. God, don't take him. I need him more than you do. Have mercy.

Feeling an abrupt and urgent need to get away from the graves, Maylene stood. Her feet dislodged a cluster of leaves that blew away. A flash of green caught her eye. There, next to Robin's lopsided headstone, were six inch-high fingers of daffodils. Maylene bent to sweep away the surrounding leaves and found several more of the broad blades, incongruously smooth and vulnerable-looking against the stony earth.

There had been no daffodils here on other springs. Someone must have planted them last fall. Who? Maylene didn't remember anyone thinning the bulb clumps around the cabin.

Looking down at the bright, hopeful spires, she felt a rush of relief to know she wasn't alone in remembering her brother. The weight of that responsibility, she realized for the first time, had been burdensome for a young and frightened child. And had remained so.

Maylene was crossing the pasture above the cabin when she saw Margaret wave from the door of the henhouse.

"The hens have started laying!" her sister called, lifting two egg-filled fists triumphantly.

It was then a bird dropped from a branch and landed on a fence rail. A phoebe. Bright-eyed and sassy as a jaybird. Maylene caught her breath. The bird was a sign—it was God's reply.

Marcus was coming home.

CHAPTER SEVENTEEN

The cold months felt interminable in camp. The Rangers wintered in the Virginia mountains, which precluded sending letters to or receiving them from Jumping Branch. Marcus had lost interest in carving and took on a new task. He fashioned a pair of snowshoes from willow branches and rawhide. They were so coveted he made several more. Thankfully, the weather was less cold than usual, but it was snowier, minimizing scouting trips. There was little to do but wait for spring.

My dear Maylene,

I don't know how or when I'll be able to get this letter mailed, but I'm lonesome tonight and thought I'd go ahead and write. I don't know when I'll get my hands on paper again. In three months, my three years will be completed. It feels more like thirty, don't it? We never thought the war would last this long.

By now our baby is nearly a year old and I don't know if I'm the father of a son or a daughter. I couldn't help but worry—I hope everything went well and you didn't suffer too much. Our baby has a beautiful mother. Have I never told you that?

Captain Thurmond was killed at Winfield, maybe you heard. Corbin and I are well. I pray that you are too.

It's hard to believe I'll see you soon and harder than ever to wait. You haven't forgotten me, have you? It's been so long.

Your loving,
Marcus

Corbin and Marcus shared the duty of watering the horses one morning, which meant shepherding them down to a nearby stream too swift to freeze and then back to their winter paddock. It was an easy task, the horses knew the routine.

Watching the horses drink, Corbin said, "The first thing I'm gonna do when I get home is take Robbie fishing. That little guy is just the right age for his first catch."

"That's the first thing you're fixin' to do?" Marcus asked. "I've got something else in mind myself."

Corbin let out a belly-laugh, his green eyes squinting over smile-elevated cheeks. "Okay, maybe fishing is the second thing. I do miss my Mary."

"You think they miss us much?"

"Hard to say. They're plenty busy with the little ones, but they've put some pretty words in the letters they've gotten to us, haven't they? I'd say they miss us more than a little...not that we deserve it."

Marcus grinned at his friend. "Dare say. I'll never know what made Maylene consider me."

His tone changed as his gaze wandered upstream. "I get to wondering sometimes—you think we've changed too much? I mean, it's been a long time. A lot's happened."

"Naw. It's like getting back in the saddle after being laid up a spell. It will all come natural, I reckon," Corbin said.

Both men turned their attention to the horses. Their conversation was getting a little personal for eye contact.

Corbin continued. "Some mornings the mud here along the creek is frozen hard as stone and the horses can scarce walk on it the way it's all roughed up from their hooves. Other times, like now, it's soft as butter. That's how we are. We're hard when we have to be, but that ain't all we are. Mary and Maylene and our little ones bring out the other side."

"I'd like to think so."

"Maylene'll soothe you when you get home. This war ain't been easy on you."

"Or anyone," Corbin added quickly.

"I've got kind of knotted up inside. I don't suppose I ever really stopped being homesick. Did you?" Marcus asked.

"Not entirely. If I was a single man, I think I might of.... But when you have a wife back home, and young'uns.... Great God, it's hard leaving them behind."

"It's a lot to ask of a man."

The dominant mare had had her fill, and Marcus pulled on her lead, directing her out of the shallow current. Free of her influence, a chestnut gelding pounded the water with a hoof and tossed his head in play.

"That it is, and I don't intend to be 'asked' again." Corbin's voice had an unfamiliar edge.

"What do you mean?" Marcus asked, turning to look the larger, dark-haired man in the eye.

"I'd pack up the family and head for Canada if I had to. I won't do this twice." Corbin moved away to retrieve the chestnut, now seeking grass in streamside brush.

Marcus was thunderstruck. Corbin, who never made a word of complaint. Cheerful, resolute Corbin. Under the surface, he carried the same smoldering anger Marcus carried, that of a man denied freedom and kin. The anger of a proud man reduced to servitude.

Blessed Jesus, Marcus thought. All this time.

By 1865, the South was spent. Funds, provisions, horses, grandfathers, fathers, young men, boys—all depleted. Richmond was seized by Union troops on the third of April. General Lee retreated as far as he was able, then, six days later, surrounded and defeated, surrendered in a quiet ceremony at the home of Wilmer McLean at a village called Appomattox Court House.

The war was over.

The news took nearly a week to reach the Rangers, and several more days of confusion followed before the company was disbanded. By then, Marcus and Corbin were seventeen days shy of discharge.

"Take your guns and gear," said Corporal Warren. "They're all the payment you'll likely see."

As soon as he got to a post office, Marcus mailed his letter to Maylene, having added at the bottom, I am on my way. It arrived after he did.

They came from the north, down the swollen Greenbrier, a straggling band of survivors. Short on horses, the men had felled a yellow poplar and made a large dugout canoe. Marcus and Corbin were among those mounted. Nine floated their way downstream, navigating with rough paddles hurriedly shaped.

The canoe was deemed too heavy for a portage at the one danger spot, Bacon's Falls. The men tensed when they heard the rising sound of cascading water. High flow protected the vessel from rocks, however, and the cumbersome canoe made the drop without capsizing. The men shouted as they paddled out of the spray and back into slower current. All that remained was to keep the nose pointed downstream—they were hours away from the confluence with New River.

Marcus found himself vigilant and jittery, unlike the others, who sang and talked, celebrating their liberty and taking full advantage of their last chance to exchange verbal jabs. He felt they were letting their guard down too soon. There were scores to settle in this land of mixed loyalties, and he wasn't about to be taken by surprise.

Late that day, Marcus was beginning to relax with fatigue when he recognized a landmark. Ahead was a gigantic rock, a sloping, flat-topped slab taller than a house, positioned on the river's flank. He'd seen it as a boy when his pa had taken Junior and him up Greenbrier River for fishing and exploration. New River was only a couple of miles away, and from there it wasn't far to Pack's Ferry, then downstream to Madam's Creek, home.

He could be at the Farley cabin soon after nightfall.

A movement caught his eye and he instinctively pulled Blackjack up. He must have imagined it. Too many months of wariness. But had he glimpsed, near the base of a rocky bluff across the river, a dark shoulder slipping back behind a flared oak trunk?

Before Marcus had time to consider further, the first shots and telltale bursts of smoke from the bluff above the massive rock put him in motion. He dismounted and used Blackjack as a shield as he unpacked his rifle. From below, he heard branches breaking as the canoe crash-landed, men yelling obscenities as they hauled themselves out.

More shots, return fire.

Good God, we've been ambushed. Must be Garten's Company—hell, haven't they gotten word? Marcus pressed his back against a trunk. Yes, he'd reloaded the rifle after shooting at—and missing—a wood duck last night.

Use it! he commanded himself.

He did not. He stood frozen, wildly thinking he was not willing to die, not here, so close to home, the war over. Die for nothing.

He heard more shouts, running feet. His men were taking flight, heading up the mountainside, away from the river. There was no fight left in any of them.

Marcus tore himself from the safety of the tree and turned to follow. Remounting Blackjack, he caught sight of blue-coated men cresting the opposite ridge, running away. He urged the horse up, up, up, putting the protection of distance and forest behind them both.

Once beyond view of the river, the men regrouped. The canoe had been pierced and was taking on water when its paddlers abandoned it. Edgar Mann was missing a button shot clean off his chest. But the men and their horses were unharmed.

New River beckoned like a promised land over Wolf Creek Mountain. The Rangers climbed to the peak and crossed part of the expansive, hilly summit before making camp for the night. They would complete the overland crossing in the morning and be damned if they weren't going to make their way home.

Marcus lay wrapped in his tattered blanket that night, looking at the star-studded sky. The last coffin nail had been driven into his experience as a soldier. Up until this day, whatever remorse he carried had been smoothed of its sharpest edges by the knowledge that he'd never failed to do what was required to keep his brothers-in-arms alive. He'd missed by one day taking that small trophy of pride home with him—now it was as sunk as the dugout canoe. He'd been a coward in the end, and his inaction could have cost a man his life.

Think about tomorrow. Maylene. Your baby. It's over.

Why didn't it feel over? He kept seeing himself pressed against the bark, like an immobile squirrel hiding from a descending hawk.

He drew an elbow over his face, shutting out the beauty of the night sky.

The final day. The Ferry. Two men headed south in the direction of Pipestem, one up the Bluestone River toward the village of Lilly, named after Marcus's ancestors. Four others turned in the Bluestone direction to pick up the Turnpike, bound for Ellison Ridge, Sand Knob, and Jumping Branch. With gathering impatience, the remainder moved along the wide New, freshly bordered with unfurling leaves.

At the mouth of Madam's Creek, Marcus turned away from the river, then looked back and reined in Blackjack when Corbin didn't follow.

"You comin'?"

"No." It took Corbin a moment to face Marcus directly. "Mary and the kids are home down the river. Jimmy Adkins told me when he joined up. Said they been there all winter."

Marcus reeled inwardly. "You known since last month and didn't say nothin'? Why didn't you say so?"

Marcus's eye bored into Corbin.

"Aw, don't be sore, Marcus. You had enough weighing on your mind. I just figured someone at home took sick or got hurt, and Mary went to help out. I've been stewing over it, but it's likely nothing to concern you."

"You didn't think I could handle it? Jesus, Corbin, you shoulda told me. The trouble could just as well be at the Farley end, and you know it. I've as much right to know as you."

"You do, but it troubled me enough I didn't see no sense in us both losing sleep. Maybe I chose wrong."

The others began edging downstream, uncomfortable to be gawking at a rift between the two men they'd never seen quarrel.

"That you did!" Marcus spun Blackjack upstream and urged him into a gallop, saying "Damn you!" when his back was turned and Corbin couldn't hear.

Little more than a mile separated him from Maylene and his child, and now he felt a new urgency to cover the ground. Why would Mary have left with her children? Had the Farley home been burned? Had Mr. Farley been killed, the family robbed? Was Maylene.... No, he must shut down his wild imaginings.

Moments later, having slowed Blackjack's pace on the rough road and given Corbin's interpretation further consideration, Marcus came to a narrow path leading to the creek bank. There he allowed himself to pause to let Blackjack drink and to make one final preparation. He was filthy and he stank. He stripped down and plunged with a shout into cold water pooled beneath a small waterfall, scrubbing his skin with sand, rubbing his face, doing what he could to clean up.

It centered Marcus to spend those minutes in Madam's Creek, the feel of fine gravel under his feet evoking memories of the stream as the wading pool, sand box, and zoo of his childhood. How many hours had he spent with Maylene and their siblings constructing miniature walls and buildings with the creek's small, rounded rocks? He could recall stone roadways across the sand. Tunnels dug with mussel shells. Rounded bark used for roofs. The pleasure of finding crawdads and salamanders. The shimmering flash of minnows. Trails left by snails across algae-covered cobbles. Marcus felt immersed in natal waters that passed through his skin as readily as between his fingers. He could trust that current to take him where it always had—to the playmate who became the woman, who became his wife.

With nothing to dry himself, he hastily climbed back into his faded gray and remounted, shivering. But sunshine and excitement joining forces with anxiety warmed him quickly. By the time he reached the lower field of the Farley farm and caught sight of the cabin chimney, Marcus felt himself vibrating like the wings of a honeybee.

Melva was collecting dandelion and mustard greens near the creek when she spied a cavalryman riding up the road. He was a slight man, bearded, on a black horse. A patch that looked of leather covered one eye. She stiffened when the man turned his horse's head. Why was this stranger coming up the lane and approaching the bridge?

The man spotted her and pulled up. Regretting she hadn't dropped behind a boulder while she had the chance, Melva stood her ground.

"Melva," spoke the man. He smiled.

The voice was familiar. But who....

"Marcus!"

Melva Farley ran toward the bridge, her basket of greens flung to the ground.

Maylene thought she heard Melva yell. She must have imagined it. Margaret might hoot or holler over something, but not Melva. Still, curiosity got the better of her, and as soon as she finished changing Jenny's diaper, Maylene asked Mama to watch the baby for a minute.

There was a man leading a black horse toward the house, Melva beside him. His smile faltered as the woman he sought stepped into the sun.

Is she ill? Why is she so thin?

The beard threw Maylene for a moment. But not the walk, not the left eye trained on her. Maylene felt what remained of fortitude drain from her like the final trickle of sap from a tapped maple. She sank onto the top step, tears pooling. Marcus had to help her up, but she gave way again so he joined her on the step. He could only hold her while she cried. What words could renounce three years of unspoken desperation? Three years of prayers, of nighttime terrors, of resentment, of emptiness, of hunger for each other.

Marcus held his weeping, shuddering wife tightly, tightly, his eyes closed against all that had gone before.

CHAPTER EIGHTEEN

Maylene lifted her face, burrowed in Marcus's neck, to find a world transformed. A veil had been pulled back from her winter-shrouded senses. Had violets thrusting their petals out of the fresh grass been so bright an hour ago? Had the afternoon been graced with songs of robins and blackbirds? Had the air carried the humus-rich scent of the warming earth? Maylene dried her face with her skirt and trembling hands, and rose unsteadily to her feet. Marcus, unwilling to let her go, kept an arm snugly around her waist as he gave one-armed hugs to Margaret and his mother-in-law.

Sara Mae sent Margaret off with a hatchet to dispense with two hens—an extravagant act—and instructed Melva to find her father and collect more greens. The family feasted that evening on fresh milk, roasted chicken, spring greens swimming in butter, and chicory coffee richly laden with cream. Lacking flour and meal, Sara Mae was at a loss for a dessert and settled on a jar of honey, passed around and around the table until it was empty, comb and all.

Marcus was restless, as if he'd forgotten how to exist indoors. He was content to let Margaret and Sara Mae dominate the conversation, as he clutched Maylene's hand with his chicken-greased fingers under the table. As soon as the honey jar was exhausted, he excused himself to check on Blackjack. Maylene sensed his ill ease.

Jenny had yet to meet her father. She had pressed her face into Margaret's, intimidated by the hubbub when Marcus arrived. Marcus had been too distracted by Maylene to force the issue. There would be time later to take his daughter in his arms. Jenny had hidden behind furniture and skirts during supper preparations, then slept through the meal.

Now she was up, and nursing in the rocker when Marcus came back inside. Marcus was too uncomfortable to approach, unused to seeing his wife's breast partially exposed in the company of his in-laws. He returned to the table, where Bob shared a jug of moonshine—frowned upon by Sara Mae but tolerated on special occasions—until Jenny had had her fill and Maylene was fully covered. Jenny stood on her mother's lap, patting Maylene's face.

"Come meet your daughter," Maylene urged.

As Marcus approached, Jenny turned a bright face toward him, and Marcus felt a clenching in his gut. He had seen Jenny's thick black hair, but he hadn't taken in her dark eyes. Now, with her face next to Maylene's, he could see that her skin was a shade darker. Her face was wide, like Maylene's, but her mouth was wider, without the fullness of her mother's lips. She looked so unlike Maylene. And even less like him.

"What a pretty little girl," he whispered without reaching for his child.

Maylene saw the momentary shock, and felt a part of her happiness stripped away like birch bark peeled by the wind.

Marcus was immediately and keenly aware of the Farley's shortage of food and the shed pounds no member of the family could conceal. Even Sara Mae had lost her youthful fullness of face and looked a decade older than when he'd last seen her. Marcus guessed the Farleys had been robbed, or "liberated of rations," but he felt it inappropriate to ask. Maylene would tell him. He'd have used the family's food poverty as his excuse if he hadn't feared hurting his father-in-law's feelings. Instead he expressed anxiety about his father. He kissed Maylene—promising to come back for her and Jenny the next day—resaddled Blackjack and left for home, less than an hour's ride at a walk.

It was a magical time, with buckeyes and poplars already attired in tender green. Sugar maples wore the reds of their new leaves, oaks pinks and peaches. Circumspect chestnuts were donned with lime halos as their buds burst open. The mountains looked as if God had blown a lungful of life across them, resuscitating them from their winter coma. Madam's Creek ran clear as glass, her small falls and riffles blending their sounds with those of songbirds voicing their evening tunes. If he hadn't been dead-tired, Marcus would have taken it all in. If he hadn't been sorely distracted.

He arrived shortly before dark, greeted his overjoyed family, ate a large wedge of corn pone, and then, justified by sleep deprivation but motivated by an intense desire to be alone, made his way to the dark cabin that had hunkered on the mountainside, voiceless and empty, for nearly two years.

"Let him go," Quentin said to his wife. "Give him time to get used to all of us again."

As stars began to dot the sky, spring peepers tuned up in the pond below. The smell of wood smoke lifted toward Broomstraw Ridge. Marcus took off his boots, wrapped himself once more in the wool blanket that had barely kept him from freezing for three years, and curled on the bed's straw tick, expecting to sleep at once. Instead he passed a particularly restless night, with fitful sleep. He was not accustomed to sleeping by himself. There were no pickets on duty.

He didn't feel safe.

They came together at last on the bed Johnny had made, under the fluffy blanket Maylene and her mother had stitched and stuffed. Serenaded by dozens of peepers, they made love. Their union gave them pleasure, to be sure, but it lacked the joyful spontaneity they had known before. They were cognizant of Jenny, sleeping on a folded blanket nearby, anxious not to wake her. And Marcus was self-conscious about his missing eye, careful that his patch not slip out of place for fear the ugly scar would disgust and frighten Maylene. Even if she couldn't make out details, there was moonlight enough for her to see that what should be there wasn't. For her part, Maylene was uncomfortable about being on her period, an aspect of female physiology she hadn't yet broached with Marcus, who, as it turned out, couldn't have been bothered less. In addition to those distractions, they felt hesitant with one another, needing time to relearn their previous closeness. Even with the encouragement of cheerful-sounding, like-minded frogs, distance imposed by so much time apart couldn't be fully bridged in one sensual evening.

But there was something else. After Marcus fell asleep, Maylene smoothed his hair, pondering the unexpected sadness that rested heavily on her chest, like a too-heavy cat curled upon her. She sensed Marcus had come home in mind and body only. His heart and soul remained somewhere distant, lost in a wild, wooded place she couldn't reach.

When she slept she dreamed she pushed thorny branches away from her shoulders and face, looking in dim light for something she needed desperately to find.

CHAPTER NINETEEN

Quentin Lilly was gradually becoming a drunk. He remained a hardworking man who hitched Pal to the wagon and went up to the woods to cut trees for firewood and fence rails. He toiled in the garden. With his powerful arms, he hoisted heavy bushel-baskets and sacks of potatoes, apples, and cornmeal. He cut, raked, and stacked hay. He remained a devoted father and husband. But chronic pain took its toll, exhausting him. In addition, he hadn't found a way to grieve for his lost sons, nor made his peace with having allowed his last words with Junior to be hot-headed ones. He knew precisely the last thing he'd said to his eldest son, "You're making a damn foolish mistake," to which Junior had answered, "Let it rest, Pa!" as he stormed off to the barn. Junior had left that night without a good-bye.

Quentin's days ended earlier, as he sought relief from fatigue and discomfort in whiskey, and he found it harder to rise with the pre-sunrise crowing of the rooster. Suzanne was unaccountably solicitous—had it been one of her children, she'd have raised Cain. Wherever there was slack, she did her best to pick it up or see that one of the girls did.

"Rachel, milk the cow this morning. Your pa's under the weather," she'd instruct as she mixed batter for johnnycakes.

Calvin and Lester, now nine and seven, gravitated in Marcus's direction. He took them hunting and fishing, began teaching them the finer points of farming. He so sternly deflected questions about his war experience, however, that the boys soon gave them up.

Calvin had a schoolmate who built a cigar-box banjo, and the instrument fascinated Calvin to the point of obsession. Marcus procured a box at Meador's Store, ordered his brother to cut a basswood sapling, and spent hours helping assemble and adjust the simple instrument. Calvin bent over the cherished invention, his thick, reddish-blond hair nearly obscuring his face, plucking and strumming with intense concentration. Marcus was confounded to hear recognizable tunes coming from the boxy banjo in a matter of days.

Marcus had little time for his brothers, however. A hundred tasks awaited him. Papa needed help cutting trees, firewood awaited splitting, there was the plowing Papa could no longer manage, the sheep were overdue for shearing, tools required repair and fence rails replacing. In addition, the cabin remained scant on furniture, including a much-needed rocking chair.

Maylene had hoped to join Marcus in many of these labors, but he would say the same things—no, it's too hot for you to be out in the sun swinging an axe, or Calvin will help me, or it won't take but a minute, I'll be back soon. He seemed to shun the companionable sharing of tasks they'd once enjoyed.

To Maylene's dismay, even Sunday mornings fell by the wayside. Marcus felt confined in the small, crowded church. He insisted on sitting on the back bench, close to the door. There were times when the congregation returned to their seats after a hymn that Marcus remained standing. After three Sundays of severe agitation, Marcus refused to return.

Maylene sometimes went home from church with her own family but not often. She felt sheepish that Marcus wasn't with her and didn't want to answer questions about him. And every week she hoped this might be the Sunday Marcus would "set a spell," read aloud to her and Jenny. Go for a walk with her in search of morels. But those Sunday afternoons didn't come.

It didn't help Marcus that the war, like mythical Hydra, refused to die. Word spread through the region that a Secessionist leader suspected of murdering a staunch Unionist during the war had been shot and killed by a group of Union veterans, one of which was Tuck Richmond, son of the first murdered man. Adding to the insult, Tuck and his friends set fire to their victim's home and outbuildings, and killed his dog.

The Secessionist was well known to Marcus. He was Jefferson Bennett, former Partisan Ranger, father of eight, assassinated at his home on Broomstraw Ridge.

The news shook the entire community but was especially hard on Marcus. It chilled him to the quick to think of Mr. Bennett surviving the hardships and risks of war only to come home and be shot point-blank as he sat waiting in the sun for his wife to finish packing a picnic lunch. It further unnerved him to learn Tuck and his father, Sam, were of the very Richmond family that had loaned him a horse when he had come home, almost too ill to ride, after his bout with typhoid fever. He would never know if Jeff Bennett had killed Sam Richmond, but it was widely known there was bad blood between the two men.

Now revenge for the second killing seemed likely, putting people on guard, and Marcus knew just the person to settle the score. He was newly returned Confederate veteran, another former Partisan Ranger, and eldest son of the latest deceased, Robert Bennett.

There would be more trouble. Marcus no longer left the farm without carrying a knife or firearm.

His edginess expressed itself in other ways. The even-tempered Marcus Maylene had known had been replaced by one easily knocked off balance. A clod of dirt sailing off a horse's hoof, a clumsy horsefly—anything that flew toward Marcus's face made him jerk his head back, throw a protective arm over his face. Even ordinary annoyances, like a horse might throw a shoe or an axe handle might break, set him off.

"Blessed Mother of God!" he shouted when the cow spilt milk.

Maylene was learning a whole new lexicon of expletives.

She did her best to believe Marcus would adapt to post-war life, that he'd come around. And she had Jenny to distract her and keep her busy.

Yet months passed with no change. Although Robert Bennett beat Tuck Richmond half to death and the score between the families appeared settled, Marcus remained, as Johnny would have said to goad Eliza into correcting him, as jumpy as a hen in a fox house. Maylene began to be lonely, missing her home on Madam's Creek. It wasn't surprising, she thought, to miss her family, but how could she miss Marcus when he was right there? She tried to be more engaged with the Lillys, with whom she and Marcus shared their evening meals, lingering over dish-washing while Marcus helped his father with the days' last chores. She tried spending more time with Marcus's teenaged sisters, who all looked up to her. She assisted them in carding and spinning wool and skutching, spinning, and weaving flax. Mending clothes.

Eliza, closest to Maylene in age, was the most receptive. With her father's strong, large-nosed face and muscular build, she might have been considered the least pretty of the Lilly sisters. But she also had her mother's generous bust, with added padding all her own, and a winning smile, the combined effect of which allowed her femininity to prevail. Her sandstone-colored hair was smooth and straight, her eyes hazel and lively. She was outgoing, talkative, and prone to laughter, much like Johnny. The entire family—Maylene included—found it easy to forgive her tendency toward bossiness.

Try as she might, however, Eliza was never able to entirely conceal her jealously of Rachel, less than two years younger. Rachel had taken her father's features and softened them beautifully. Her wide face was a perfect match for her generous and wavy red hair. She turned Quentin's muscular form into a fit, curvaceous female shape. She added a dimple to her left cheek. She adopted her mother's blue eyes. There was something adorable about her appearance that made older folks chuckle and girls her age envious. It only provoked Eliza that Rachel was oblivious. She thought she was perfectly ordinary-looking, and paid little attention to her looks. She was a girl of action who threw herself wholeheartedly into each task, a girl blessed with seemingly boundless energy. And she was Margaret Farley's best friend.

By now Maylene had discovered endearing aspects of the older sisters and was beginning to coax the younger two out of their shyness. As a group, however, the Lilly sisters drove her to distraction with their bickering. She became exhausted trying to sort out why Eliza wasn't talking to Rachel, what secret Louella was keeping from Vesta, and when or if she should play peacemaker. She wished the sisters had young men for distraction, but there was a woeful shortage at the moment.

The sisters proved helpful as babysitters, as did Calvin and Lester. The boys often played with Jenny while Maylene gardened or split wood. It gave her a pang to watch the natural way they teased and cuddled their niece. Marcus was kind to Jenny but in a distant way. He was so reserved and polite it set Maylene's teeth on edge.

Does he really think... No, how could he? He *knows* me.

It was good she couldn't read his thoughts, which were dank and chaotic much of the time. Marcus remained unable to put the war—which shadowed him in nightmares—behind him. And he couldn't get past Jenny's appearance. It was why he pushed himself so hard. Only by staying constantly busy and exhausting himself each day could he keep the tentacles of his imaginings from constricting his lungs. Only then could he turn onto his side at night and sleep.

He had always trusted Maylene above all others. She had been the beacon in his darkest times as a soldier, the light that had kept him moving forward, doing what had to be done so that he could survive and return to her. He had thought of her every day and night, using his abiding faith in her to uphold him when every other bastion of faith was lost.

Now, when he looked at Jenny, he felt that faith shaken. How could she possibly be his child? Hadn't Maylene written that their baby was expected in mid-March? Why had Jenny come at the end of the month? Where had she gotten her dark hair and complexion, the features of her face so unlike his or Maylene's? Unlike his parents or any of his siblings, unlike any of Maylene's kin. But if she wasn't his, then whose?

Marcus chased his questions around and around, like a cat in pursuit of its own tail.

Had Maylene been forced by another man? Rape was not such a rarity during the war. No, he could make no sense of that. She was a fighter and would have never submitted. The struggle would have left her emotionally scarred. He would be able to tell.

Had her grief over his departure affected her reason, sent her into another man's arms? That made no sense either. With the exception of her brief interest in Amos, Maylene wasn't the fickle sort, nor the flirtatious type, and when would she have had the opportunity to be alone with a man? She was constantly with family.

Marcus could find no answer, nor could he find a way to ask Maylene. Instead he drove himself with punishing work, pushing the war and his wife and daughter away, all three being dire threats to a fortress even a baby could knock to pieces.

CHAPTER TWENTY

One late-summer morning a yellow jacket flew into the cabin, landing on the floor near Jenny where she sat on a blanket banging two wooden spoons together.

"Dat?" The toddler reached for it before Marcus, seated above her and snaring his last spoonful of grits, could intervene.

Jenny jumped with a look of surprise, opened her mouth wide, and let out a paint-peeling scream.

Instead of reaching for his daughter, Marcus bolted for the door as if an entire nest of hornets was after him. Dumbfounded, Maylene came around the table and picked up her wailing child.

"Marcus?"

He was gone.

Marcus climbed all the way up Broomstraw Ridge before he collapsed—heart pounding, sweat streaming—onto a boulder at the outcrop overlooking the valley far below. Miniaturized from where he sat, New River looked insubstantial and mild, making its crooked way north, its rapids reduced to faint white lines.

He let himself fall back across the warm rock to study the sky, strewn with white clouds. A monarch butterfly coasted above him, reminding him summer was nearly over. Soon there would be a steady stream of the bright orange butterflies heading south. He and Maylene used to lie like this and count them on September afternoons.

He closed his eye as a wave of disgust swept over him. I've become the Hooded Thief, he thought.

He saw himself stealing into the lives of his wife and daughter at night, removing morsels of their happiness one by one. How long would it be before their world collapsed entirely, deprived of the foundation of trust and love it was supposed to rest upon? He wanted to spit out the poison within him that made him unable to join in his daughter's laughter, unable to flirt and banter with his wife, eject that bitter bile that kept him coiled like a snail shell within himself, armed and ever on the alert, as if he remained a picket guarding a deserted camp.

How was he going to heal himself when he couldn't look at Jenny without a cold hand closing over his heart?

He stayed away all day. By the time Marcus returned to the cabin, it was dusk and Jenny was asleep. Maylene stepped onto the newly finished porch and gave him a questioning look as he lowered himself onto a step. She went back inside for a cup of coffee, which she placed in his hands before sitting down next to him.

"I heard an old man trapped in a burning house. I heard a horse scream when...." He cradled the coffee, wouldn't look at her.

Maylene waited. She placed a hand on his back. "Shall we ever talk about it?"

"I killed a man. Maybe others."

Maylene drew in a short, sharp breath and told herself to bank her emotions, like snuffing the bedtime fire. "I'm confident you had no choice."

"I tried to spare them. I tried not to hate."

"That don't surprise me."

She could feel his struggle as if it were her own, and still she waited as he teetered on the brink of breaking, shattering into a thousand pieces that neither she nor he would be able to reassemble. He took a long, shuddering inhalation.

"I failed at both. No, we shan't talk of it."

"Then I'll not ask. But if you change your mind, know it won't be a burden to me."

Marcus rose from the steps and started for the barn. Then he stopped and turned back.

"I'm sorry."

Maylene meant to say, I'm sorry, too. Instead she said, "I know," as if the words had volition of their own.

Forced to shorten his work hours as the days shrank, Marcus began getting better acquainted with Jenny and couldn't help taking genuine delight in the bright little girl.

"Papa," she said, lifting her arms in invitation to be held. He would scoop her up and kiss a plump cheek.

"Pay horsey," she said, wanting to be bounced on his knee.

Marcus complied.

It was difficult to roughhouse with a toddler and keep an eyepatch in place. Inevitably it slipped, revealing the ragged pink-and-white scar over the crater of the socket. Before Marcus could re-cover it, Jenny had her hand on it.

"What dat?" she queried, patting.

"That's where my eye used to be. I lost it."

Jenny giggled. "Where it go?"

Her question made Marcus laugh, and he rarely wore the patch in the cabin after that. It took Maylene a couple of weeks to get used to the chicken-foot-like substitute for the lively brown eye she couldn't help missing, but like all shocks this insult to her senses wore off. It wasn't long before she didn't notice whether Marcus covered the scar or not.

Marcus may have been warming up to Jenny, but with Maylene he continued to be reserved. Their lovemaking felt mechanical to her and left her unsatisfied. Marcus would thank her afterward, as if she had passed him a bowl of peas at supper, before turning away. Which made her feel like slapping him, although she wasn't sure why. Her womb remained as unreceptive as a closed spruce cone, she did not conceive

Day by day, Maylene's sadness turned to resentment. She would think, I waited three years for this? A husband who approaches me as he would a copperhead? Who won't look me in the eye?

This Marcus wasn't the same one she had known and loved all her life. She was so tired of missing that Marcus, and she blamed this Marcus for taking him away from her. She began to return Marcus's aloofness with an equal measure of her own.

Marcus focused on particulars. He was determined Maylene wouldn't have a winter like the last. Her still-gaunt form bothered him, as if it were an indictment on his ability to provide. He had adapted to one-eyed aiming and taken down a doe. Due largely to his efforts, the Lilly garden had yielded a great bounty of produce, and the corn crop was adequate for meal and feed. Marcus and his siblings, with some help from Maylene, had gathered the usual harvest of nuts from the woods. Two hogs had been slaughtered, a steer would be next. Threshed wheat grains had returned from Charlton's Mill in flour sacks on Pal's back. Without the demand for war rations, flour was finally available for bread and biscuits again.

At Maylene's request, Marcus created a rolling pin. Maylene dipped her hands in the soft wheat flour, savoring the feel of it, and went to work. Marcus said it was the best apple pie he'd ever tasted, and it was all he could do not to thrust his face right down through the warm crust like a pig in a trough.

It galled Marcus, however, that part of the corn harvest was being processed into moonshine. He clashed with Quentin over it, but gave up the fight when his mother sided with her husband.

Suzanne said, "You see as well as I do the strain on his face when he sets down for supper. He's spent by then, just plain wore out. If he needs to put that leg up and drink the pain away, I'm not inclined to stand in his way. We can spare the corn for that."

The family was fortunate in that Quentin was never an angry drunk. Instead he was sentimental, groggy, almost desperate for his wife to stay near. And near Suzanne hovered, offering a pillow under the still-swollen knee and her solicitous presence as each day drew to its close.

"Honor thy father and thy mother."

Marcus made his father an exquisite walnut cane, carved with entangled vines. He drew the line at tending the still.

Marcus was trying. He ached to feel close to Maylene again, to chip away the stony crypt he lay within, buried alive. There were moments, as when Maylene pulled those two pies from the oven, when a shaft of light got through.

Marcus recited from Maylene's memorized letter, I'm saving a thousand kisses for you.... I love our baby already....

When that tactic faltered, he turned to his fantasy life for help. He set aside Maylene's failure to conceive as evidence of his own infertility—and another indication that Jenny wasn't his—and imagined that their baby had been born dead. Maylene, in her anguish, had found another baby to mother, although whose he couldn't guess. But orphans were not unusual, especially during the war. Maylene must have wanted so fiercely to believe the adopted baby was her own that she had convinced herself, erased all memory of the first baby, his baby. The Farleys, alarmed by Maylene's state of mind, had accepted the ploy, taking Jenny in as their own.

This fragile concoction calmed Marcus's inner turbulence, despite the fact he knew he grasped at straws. It helped him set aside the dagger-pointed question that had been bleeding him with tiny cuts since he first saw Jenny's upturned face.

Like all self-deceptions, however, it had a limited shelf life.

CHAPTER TWENTY-ONE

Rumors of theft began to circulate. In effect, the larceny was a form of organized crime, legitimized by the government's attempt to collect goods once owned by the Confederacy. Unfortunately, some of those who volunteered for the task were overly zealous. Instead of confiscating only horses and firearms, they robbed their neighbors blind.

Maylene thought reports of men carrying away foodstuffs, clothing, and jewelry—along with horses and guns—were exaggerated. Marcus found them entirely believable, having seen such thorough household thievery during the war.

It wasn't long before Mary and Corbin related just such a case not far from their home. One of the perpetrators, attempting to cross an exceptionally high creek on a stolen horse, drowned wearing three overcoats. Contributing to the man's demise was his stuffing of the coat pockets with jewelry, flatware, and coins. The unburdened horse survived and went home.

Marcus became so worried about losing the horses that he built a small paddock in the woods where he kept Pal and Blackjack by day, turning them out to graze in the pasture by night. He began storing his rifle and pistol in a haystack, returning them to the cabin at dusk.

Maylene hoped the settling of the Richmond-Bennett feud would be the last Union-Confederate shedding of blood. But it was impossible to know. While it saddened her to see the erosion of trust in what had been a close-knit community, it was especially painful to see it in Marcus. She remembered him as an introverted but open-hearted boy, who expected to like everyone he met. Maylene feared the jagged wound left by the war would be a long time scabbing over, not only for Marcus but for the entire world she knew.

It was fall when the men came, three of them, armed and unsmiling.

"We understand there is a Rebel veteran here," said their spokesman, a dark-haired, paunchy man with spectacles and mustache. He wore a Union uniform. "We're here to claim government property."

"That would be Marcus," Suzanne answered in an equally unfriendly voice. Do they not know about Quentin? "He's in the barn."

Lord, don't let him lose his head, she prayed, thinking of Marcus's shortened fuse.

The mule tipped him off. Marcus looked up from trimming Nettie's hooves. He knew at once.

The mustached man wasted no time. "Marcus Lilly? We're here to collect your horse and rifle."

Marcus dropped the hooked knife into the box of grooming tools more forcefully than he meant to. He placed a hand on Nettie's back and fixed his eye on the stranger, thinking it likely he was under Garten's command and had heard about the final skirmish.

"I come down the Greenbrier in a dugout canoe. It was shot full of holes and sunk, taking my rifle with it. I come home with nothing but the clothes on my back."

The men exchanged looks. "This mule all you got?"

"See for yourself."

The men left with the mule and Quentin's old musket. The Lillys felt they'd gotten off easy.

"I hate to see Nettie go," Quentin said, "but that ole girl is just about wore out. I didn't expect to get more than another year of work outta her anyhow."

It was the first time Marcus felt proud of a lie.

Late that winter Corbin Radcliff made an appearance at the Farley farm. There wasn't one among them who didn't know it was bad news when he appeared at the door, his face uncharacteristically clouded.

"Who?" asked Bob, afraid for Mary.

"It's Sallie. Scarlet fever. We got Robbie out of the house right quick. Put him up with my aunt and uncle. Doc Williams said we done all we could. He said don't have no regrets." Corbin landed hard in a chair, his little speech having sucked the faint vitality from him.

Shock dropped Sara Mae to another seat. "Dear God. How is Mary holding up?"

"She's doing her best. She wants to come here next week and stay 'til the baby's born. The burial's planned for Friday if the weather holds. We thought afternoon, to give you time. My aunt will put you up that night. If there's a storm, come as soon as you can. We'll hold off."

"We'll be there." Bob stepped with instinctive protectiveness toward his wife.

"Oh, Corbin, our darling Sallie." As the news sank in, tears brimmed in Sara Mae's eyes. Margaret and Melva held each other.

Corbin began to overheat. Three women on the verge of weeping made him feel like a cat dropped into a kennel of hounds. He gave his father-in-law a panicked look. "I'd best be getting back."

"Won't you stay for a bite to eat?" Sara Mae protested, but vaguely, as if unaware of her words.

Bob understood. "No, hon, Corbin has a long ride back and not much daylight. Mary must want him home." He escorted a grateful Corbin to the door.

"Thank you, Mrs. Farley," Corbin almost forgot to say. "I got plenty of jerky in the saddle bag."

"Margaret, run fetch Corbin some apples. Be sure to get some yellow ones for your sister," Bob said, putting his hand on the back of Corbin's neck as the men stepped out.

The ground was snow-free and the mules well-fed. Maylene and Marcus left Jenny with her Lilly grandparents and piled into the Farley wagon—which carried three heavily wrapped human shapes on the seat and three on a mound of straw—for the nine-mile trip down the river to New Richmond. The family made up a somber entourage under a sagging gray sky.

They found Mary ashen and dry-eyed, wearing the haunted look of the exhausted. Maylene wondered if her sister had slept at all since Sallie's death three days earlier. It was unlikely she'd been eating either, although hard to tell as she was nearly nine months pregnant. Mary was already packed for the return trip, clearly in need of some time away from the home where her child had died.

The service was a brief grave-side affair on a gusty, snow-spitting afternoon. Only Corbin's determination had gotten through the frozen inches of soil and readied the site, set within a low iron fence marking the Radcliff family cemetery. Like most mountain burial plots, it sat high above the surroundings—at the crest of a pasture. It offered a sweeping view of New River.

Marcus, with strangers around him, felt his pulse picking up speed. The Farley and Radcliff women cried quietly. Bob blew his nose on a handkerchief. It was Corbin who broke down completely, sobbing as the little pine casket was lowered into the ground. And it was then that Marcus, who had slipped an arm around Maylene, began taking quick, shallow breaths. He felt internal pressure, as if a suffocating animal were trapped within him, as if it was his heart, not lungs, that sought air. It was a heart pressed into a space too small, guarded in its love for brothers-in-arms who might die or desert at any moment, denied its natural compassion for Northerners who might have to be maimed or killed. But it hadn't failed to love Corbin, who had guided Marcus through the tedium and trauma of their shared years with a steadfast, unearthly calm. Seeing him shattered unnerved Marcus in an abrupt and unanticipated way. He felt Corbin's pain crumble the support beneath him like an undertow pulling him into the ocean of his own pain—drowning him dead.

Maylene turned toward her husband, placing a hand on his free arm, but before she could speak he broke away. He strode to Corbin, embraced him, and bolted for the bottom of the long slope.

Maylene caught her father's eye, and he made a slight shake of his head. Don't go. That's a man who needs to be alone.

Maylene let Marcus be.

The baby was a boy and he had a familiar look. He arrived on the ninth of March, and Maylene wondered if she alone took note of the date, the same one carved into Robin's stone on the mountainside above Madam's Creek.

"The Lord taketh away, and the Lord giveth," she thought, as she sought Marcus with news of CJ's arrival. She found her husband in the barn, pitching hay in the failing light of dusk.

"Papa's here, so come in soon as you can. He's playing with Jenny and says he'll put on his hat when she starts yawning, and he'll high-tail it for home when she starts to squall."

Marcus swung the fork and let another mound of hay fly from loft to stall. "Your pa's always been a sensible man. Everything all right?"

"Yes, it's a boy, and Mary is well enough. His name is CJ, for Corbin James, and Papa says he favors Corbin."

Reporting the news—that the parentage of Corbin James was obvious to all—Maylene felt the same twinge of envy she'd known at the receiving end.

"Good to hear!" Marcus leaned on the pitchfork handle and gave Maylene a rare smile before resuming his work.

Maylene watched him for a moment, admiring the fluid motions of his shoulders and arms. He'd shed his coat, despite the evening chill. "Papa said Mary broke down and bawled after CJ had his first little cry and got wrapped up. She said she feels like she has a hole the size of a goose egg in her heart and maybe little CJ will make it not hurt so bad. Mama told Pa it was the first time she seen Mary cry over Sallie since her burying day."

Marcus paused again.

"She don't like to show her pain, never has."

"I got an idea just now after talking with Pa. Jenny still doesn't have a middle name. What if we make it Sallie Mae?"

"Huh. Jenny Sallie Mae Lilly. That's a right mouthful, ain't it?"

"You don't like it."

"I didn't say that. I'm just trying it out. When she's ornery, 'Miss Jenny Sallie Mae!'"

Now Maylene was smiling. He'd already said yes.

One benefit came from the sledgehammer blow of Sallie's death. Margaret, now eighteen, met a seventeen-year-old cousin of Corbin's—Harris Keeney—at the funeral. Young enough to escape the draft, he had skated through the war unscathed. As soon as the spring mud subsided, Harris began riding, freshly washed and whistling, to Madam's Creek on Sunday mornings.

CHAPTER TWENTY-TWO

That summer, Suzanne Lilly announced it was time for her two younger daughters, Vesta and Louella, to be baptized. The occasion called for new dresses, and homespun cloth would not suffice. With some prodding, Quentin grudgingly agreed to dip into the family's small income from wool for the purchase of fabric.

Maylene took pleasure assisting Vesta in the creation of her dress, lavender with dark-blue stripes. Suzanne and Louella joined forces on a rich blue, trimmed with lace. Lacking a sewing machine, their labors went slowly, but it was pleasant to sit together sewing on the porch while tomatoes and squash swelled in the garden and a bullfrog's droll bass voice sounded from the pond.

Maylene and Suzanne were determined Marcus would attend the service. Outnumbered, he relented. He bathed and put on Junior's white shirt, freshly starched, for the occasion. He trimmed his beard and mustache, shaved the perimeter. He groomed Pal and Blackjack.

Maylene was struck by how handsome he looked when Marcus led the horses up from the barn.

"I have a good-looking husband," she said as he helped his mother mount.

Marcus gave her rear a swat, and Maylene realized it was the first playfulness he'd aimed in her direction since he'd been home. A flutter of happiness, like the fleet passage of a hummingbird, went through her.

Her mother-in-law sent Maylene back inside to hurry the girls along. She found Vesta and Louella primping in front of a small mirror propped against a pickle jar on the dining table. They looked fresh as bridesmaids in their new dresses, yet their similarities of appearance ended there.

Vesta strongly resembled both Marcus and their mother, at least her face and slight form did. Her hair, however, was her father's, and despite her daily efforts to contain it, it perpetually threatened—in a riot of red—to entirely overtake her shy visage guarded only by a pair of blazing blue eyes, which stood out defiantly, resisting encroachment.

Louella, the youngest daughter, had taken stock of the traits of parents and grandparents and made careful selections. Her hair, silky and straight like Suzanne's, was neither blond nor red, but the bronzy gold of beech leaves in autumn. Her wide face tapered to her mother's pointed chin, forming a lovely heart shape. Her eyes were green, her lips full and wide. Her skin was incapable of forming a blemish. She was, quite simply, a beautiful girl. And she knew it. From an early age she had carried herself with a certain coquettish confidence her sisters found uppity and tiresome.

Suzanne had seen Louella at birth for the belle she was. She and Quentin had intended to name her Ruth Ann, but Suzanne, holding her three-day-old seventh baby on her lap, said, "Just look at her. *Ruth Ann* don't fit her at all. She's *Louella*, plain as day."

Quentin, having recovered from the disappointment of not adding another boy to his workforce, nodded. "I believe you're right, Suze. Ain't she a pretty little thing."

On their baptismal Sunday fourteen years later, Vesta, pinned back her unruly mop of hair and let a resigned glance fall on her younger sister. She wasn't about to tell Louella how stunning she looked.

But Louella, brushing her billowing mane, had the generosity—or smugness—to say, "Vesta, you look right nice in that pretty dress."

With Louella, one was never quite sure.

Bob and Sara Mae had insisted on lending the wagon, Bob having gone to the trouble of installing the rarely used second seat, as well as the roof erected for the hottest, snowiest, or rainiest days, or, as in this case, the most special of occasions. The Lilly family made its way—some members walking, some riding—to the Farley farm to pick up the decked-out wagon and continue to the church in style. If anyone found the sight of new dresses and a borrowed wagon prideful, so be it. To Suzanne, it was simple celebration.

After the worship service, the congregation had to go down to the New to find enough water for the dunking, Madam's Creek being too low. The day was not overly warm. Everyone covered the quarter-mile in high spirits, a baptism being a notch below a wedding in festive appeal.

Paster Mullens was somber as he recited, "I baptize thee in the name of the Father, the Son, and the Holy Spirit." But the onlookers hooted and cheered as the girls, in turn, came sputtering and smiling out of the water, lifted by Mullens' aging back and spindly arms. The ceremony ended with a raucous rendition of "Down to the Sacred Wave," chosen because it was short enough that everyone knew the words by heart.

Gaiety and reverence had never been mutually exclusive for these Baptists, and they were beginning to come uncorked now that post-war peace was taking hold.

As Marcus and Maylene left the river bank, Maylene looked back at Margaret and Harris, trailing the group. It amused her how their shapes mirrored those of her parents, one short and roundish, the other tall and rail-lean.

She turned to Marcus. "What do you think?"

"I'd say that boy's in way over his head."

"Pretty smitten, isn't he?"

"I'd say. How about Margaret?"

"She rides him pretty hard, but I think it's her way of flirting."

"Good for her, then. She looks like her old uppity self again."

Maylene couldn't help thinking Johnny would have gone toe-to-toe with Margaret, never letting her get the better of him. Poor Harris truly was in over his head, but happily so.

Marcus said, "Your pa wants to rob the hives tomorrow. He asked me to help. I'll ride down after breakfast."

"That's welcome news! I'll have some biscuit dough ready when you get home. I'm hungry just thinking of hot biscuits with butter and honey."

Maylene was pleased. It could only benefit Marcus to spend time with his father-in-law. She'd always thought her pa's quiet nature had a calming effect on everyone around him.

Marcus was quiet, giving Maylene the suspicion he was working up to telling her something further.

"I thought you might come along. Bring Jenny and ride down with me."

She had to know. "Is that what Papa said?"

"No, it's my idea."

Marcus shot her a quick grin, and she felt another flurry of wingbeats within her, the soft hope of life returning to normal. And it was that softness that allowed her to resist the temptation to say, Praise God, it's a miracle! My husband has done asked me to come along.

She said instead, "I'd like that. I'll make the biscuits there and bring some home."

But the smile she meant to return to Marcus didn't form on her face, as if her hope wasn't yet strong enough to break the surface.

Quentin had driven the wagon down from church to river, grateful for the seat from which to watch the proceedings. His daughters—two dry, two wet—were arranging themselves in the back. Calvin was passing Jenny up to Lester. Marcus had taken his mother's arm to assist her onto the front seat when someone seized his own arm. He turned to find the unappealing face, incongruously contrasting with a yellow bonnet, of the dreaded Mrs. Nivens.

"Marcus Lilly!" she crowed. "I've been wanting to commend you. Such a good man. We all admire you for adopting that precious little squaw-baby of Maylene's."

Maylene, who had just taken her seat behind Quentin, felt as if she'd been kicked in the stomach by one of Pal's gigantic hooves. Her next breath was a faint gasp.

Marcus blanched nearly as white as his shirt. "Adopt? Why would I adopt my own child?"

Mrs. Nivens went slack-jawed. "Well! We just thought… She looks so…"

Marcus levitated onto the added, backward-facing seat next to Maylene, his jaws clenched like Spit refusing the bit. Quentin put the mules in motion, leaving Mrs. Nevins standing uncharacteristically speechless. Giving her a sidelong glance, Maylene thought the woman's small-eyed, puckered face resembled a rat's.

"Don't pay that woman no mind," Quentin said. "She don't know nothin' but nonsense."

Those were the only words spoken by the quartet of married couples. The rest of the family, oblivious to the brief drama, soon picked up the mood, their own conversations trailing off.

The trip was endless. Marcus sat so immobile Maylene thought, "pillar of salt." He held his hands in fists, his face as rigid as a rifle barrel. Suzanne was the same. Maylene was struck by how similar the back-to-back, mother-and-son postures of anger were, how alike their faces.

They've both turned against me, she thought. Neither looked at her. Neither offered a word of consolation.

Maylene was frantic not to cry, but the hurt was too much. Tears began spilling down her face and onto the collar of her dress.

'We all admire you....' So that's what they think, that Jenny isn't his baby. That I was unfaithful. That he is a valiant husband finding it in his heart to forgive me but too ashamed to come back to church. All this time, that's what they've been thinking. Squaw-baby? Just what does that woman and her pack of gossips think, that a contingent of Shawnee have come back from the dead and set up camp on the other side of Broomstraw?

Maylene wondered how many poison-tipped tongues wagged behind the smiles that greeted her on Sunday mornings. She thought of the progress she and Marcus had made, starting with their quiet winter together. It wasn't much, but it was something. She pictured him slowly climbing a cliff toward her, inch by inch. Now he'd lost his handholds. She could see him spiraling downward through space.

It was too much. The tears flowed faster, running in rivulets down her cheeks.

Walk faster, mules, please!

Louella and Rachel sat on one side, resting their backs against the rough boards of the wagon's short bed, with Vesta and Eliza on the other. They had to bend their knees to make room for their legs and pull their skirts over top for modesty's sake. And there sat Maylene above them, making a spectacle of herself and despising the backward-facing seat.

Rachel could stand the tension no longer. "What's *wrong*, Maylene?"

"It ain't none of your business!" Marcus answered before Maylene could speak.

Maylene turned her face away from all of them, and the four sisters, unaccustomed to seeing their sister-in-law cry and unused to being snapped at by their brother, in graceful unison shifted their attention to the wagon's rear, snubbing Marcus and supporting Maylene by averting their gazes.

"Mama!" Jenny had been with her young uncles, whose legs dangled over the laid-down wagon tailgate. She now clambered forward in search of her favorite lap. "Play pattycake!"

She took her mother's hands and clapped them together.

"Not now, Baby," Maylene answered in a strangled voice.

Eliza, bless her heart, reached for her squaw-baby niece.

When the overloaded wagon reached the Farley farm, Maylene's urge to eject herself and make a sprint for the shelter of home was overpowering. Instead she sprang past Marcus to help unhitch the mules and release them into the pasture. As Quentin and Suzanne mounted Pal, she took aim at the creek and beat everyone back across the bridge, anxious to be away before her family could catch up and see her like this.

Marcus, despite appearing to have turned to wood, was in the midst of his own cyclone of thoughts. His carefully constructed house of cards, in one fell swoop, had come tumbling down.

Of course she's Maylene's daughter. Of course she's not mine. Any fool can see that.

His mind writhed, searching an explanation. Had Maylene taken a lover that first year he was away, someone who had waited impatiently in the wings for him to recover and return to duty so the two of them could pick up where they'd left off?

No, no, no, no!

He mustn't think so. It would drive him mad.

He wanted to take Maylene by the shoulders and pin her to the seatback until he forced the truth from her.

CHAPTER TWENTY-THREE

W hen the sorry procession came at last to the Lilly home, Suzanne turned to her eldest daughter. "Eliza, we'll be watching Jenny this afternoon. See that she gets something to eat, and she'll be needing a nap. Maylene's not feeling well."

Eliza knew full well something else was up, but she also knew by her mother's tone this was not the time to ask. She lowered Jenny to Calvin's waiting arms.

"Want to hear my banjo?" Calvin asked.

Jenny bounced with excitement. "Bando!"

"Come on then. Let's play some songs 'til dinner."

Maylene wanted to thank her mother-in-law, but feared she would unravel completely if she attempted to speak. She followed Marcus's rapidly receding form up the hill to their cabin, taking her time.

Let him stew in his own juices.

Maylene's heart beat too fast to attribute to the climb. Short of breath, her mouth became chalky. She felt every way her body had joined her swirling mind in anticipation of a showdown. God help us, she prayed as she came through the door.

He whirled on her like a falcon.

"Tell me, Maylene!" His face was twisted with anguish, his voice rough. "You have to tell me the truth!" Although he made no move toward her, it was the first time Maylene sensed he wished to strike her.

She felt herself coiled inside, so tightly the band was ready to snap. As she spoke, the coil unwound, faster and faster. "The truth? You want to know the truth? It's as plain as the nose on your face!"

Her volume was rising. She had never once yelled at Marcus, and she was getting close. "How can you be so ready to believe the worst about me? I have never once...."

Rapid footsteps on the porch. Suzanne Lilly came through the open door with a book under one arm. She slammed it with such force onto the table that Maylene jumped. It was the family Bible, and Maylene couldn't help wince at the disrespectful treatment.

"Sit!" Suzanne commanded with such force they both sat at once.

Suzanne stood over them, her petite form enlarged with something fearsome brewing within. "Put your hands on the Bible and swear you will never tell another living soul what I'm about to tell you."

Marcus and Maylene exchanged stunned looks. Each placed a hand on the Bible. Their hands avoided touching as if contact would instigate combat.

Still uncoiling, and the situation appearing absurd, Maylene tightened the muscles around her mouth in a supreme effort not to smile, worse yet, cut loose with a fit of hysterical laughter. Had Ma Lilly robbed a bank? Rustled some steers?

"You swear?" Suzanne was dead serious.

Maylene nodded.

"Yes, Ma. I swear." Marcus didn't look like laughter was in his repertoire at the moment.

Satisfied, Suzanne sat down on the bench next to her son. Turning to him, she took a deep breath that she let out with four words, "Jenny is your child."

"How would you know that?"

"She looks exactly like her grandfather."

Maylene caught on before Marcus did.

"What do you mean? Which one?" Marcus asked impatiently. "She don't look like Pa or Mr. Farley."

Suzanne amended her statement. "She is the spitting image of your father."

"But...."

Marcus became still. He fixed a look on his mother that Maylene could describe only as pure loathing.

CHAPTER TWENTY-FOUR

How could she possibly make him understand?

Suzanne and Joseph had grown up much as Maylene and Marcus, sharing play and exploration. It was a friendship as vigorous and natural as a sprouting acorn.

Suzanne intended to marry her childhood companion, and grew exasperated with his reticence by the time she turned seventeen. Although she wasn't as pretty as some of the girls, she had luxurious honey-colored hair, brilliant blue eyes, and a pixieish charm. She also possessed the kind of figure boys found impossible to ignore, and she was confident of her ability to use it to her advantage. It was Joseph—quick-witted, dark, and unquestionably handsome— she wanted, and the sooner he proposed the sooner she would be rid of the attentions of other local boys, who she found pitifully unappealing.

Her flirting went a step too far.

The setup was berry-picking. She led Joseph and her mother to believe her friend Betty was coming along. Betty knew nothing of it. Suzanne's goal that day was to get Joseph to kiss her. He would want more, and she felt sure a proposal would follow in short order. It seemed a simple plan.

She met up with Joseph on a July afternoon on Brooks Mountain, high above New River, across and downstream from the mouth of Madam's Creek. And they did pick blackberries. Joseph was nervous, blindsided by Betty's absence. It didn't help that Suzanne found a dozen ways to touch him, brushing his arm with hers when they reached for the same berry, touching his hand when they dropped berries into the basket. She wore a dress she'd nearly outgrown and made sure her cleavage was visible every time she bent over a low cane, the low berries being her particular quarry that day. She teased and laughed, giddy with faith in the success of her scheme.

She was relentless.

But Joseph resisted the bait, seemingly focused entirely on the goal of filling the generous basket. Upon completion of that task, Suzanne retreated with the harvest to the shade of a young oak, where she reclined on the ground and slaked her thirst with the shiny fruits. She expected Joseph to join her. Instead, he continued picking berries, eating each one.

Suzanne quickly became impatient. "Come over here and give me a hand up, will you?"

"As you wish."

He wiped his juice-stained hands on his pants before extending an arm. Suzanne clasped his hand and pulled, but instead of helping her up, Joseph dropped to all fours. He grasped her by the wrists and loomed over her, frowning.

"What are you doing?"

"Trying to decide if I'm going to make the mistake of kissing you."

Joseph's dark eyes were devoid of their usual warmth. Nevertheless, Suzanne flicked away the warning signs like a bothersome mosquito. She guessed he was teasing and concluded the time was ripe for coyness. "What makes you think I want you to?"

"You've made it rather clear, you shameless girl."

Suzanne stiffened. "What did you call me?"

"Shameless! It ain't proper, us being up here alone like this, and you know it. Look me in the eye and tell me again how Betty took sick!"

"I'll tell you nothing 'til you get your hands off me. Let me up!"

Suzanne tried to pull her arms free, but found herself firmly trapped. She felt her pulse pounding in her temples as her anger flared. She considered the option of kneeing Joseph in the chest but didn't want to risk exposing herself, especially after his insult.

He leaned in, putting his face close to hers. It was strangely expressionless. "Don't rush me, Suzanne. You've been toying with me all afternoon. Don't expect me to do your bidding."

She and Joseph had had their share of spats over the years, but this was different. Suzanne's anger had boiled over into sputtering rage. How dare he pin her to the ground like a mouse in an owl's stranglehold.

"Let me up or I'll skin you alive!"

"Is this how you behave with other boys?"

She saw disgust on his face, then, as he released her wrists. *Other boys?* She thought she would tell him there were no other boys. Instead, Suzanne reared up and hit Joseph in the face, connecting with a crunching sound. Blood splashed out of his nose, onto her dress.

Joseph reeled backward, staggering onto his feet.

"Ow! Damn it, Suzanne, you busted my nose. Damn you to Hell!" He took a step away and investigated gingerly with one hand.

"Serves you right!" She had scrambled upright. She grabbed the berry basket and ran, down the steep mountain path, with the speed of a doe.

Close to home, she stopped and took stock of the situation. How was she going to explain the bloody dress? She took it off and rinsed it in the summer-low stream the path bordered. Better, but a stain remained.

Already ashamed of her lie, she landed on another. She wriggled back into the wet dress, removed most of the remaining berries from the basket, picked a rounded stone out of the streambed, and hammered the basket flat. Then she returned a few of the berries to the misshapen basket and went home.

She arrived visibly shaken and tearful. She told her mother she had been running on the way back down, after sending Joseph and

Betty on their way. She had fallen on the basket, crushing it and staining her dress with the berries. Worried about the damage to her dress, she had tried to wash it before the stain set. She half expected her mother to scoff at the absurd fabrication, but the fib was a complete success, the purple bruise that appeared on her knuckles adding credence to the story. Her mother's sympathy made Suzanne's guilt all the worse.

Much more painful than guilt, however, was a combination of heartbreak and outrage. Joseph had not only angered but frightened her, and she blamed him far more than herself. Why had he been so odd and distant? Why couldn't he have offered a kiss and held her hand as they walked home, as any normal boy would do?

With unusual willpower for a teen, Suzanne hid her suffering from her family, using the barn or woods for refuge when she needed to cry. And cry she did for the ruination that had come of her hopes and schemes.

The closeness she and Joseph had shared for years was as broken as the berry basket.

Ten months later, Suzanne attended a communal meal and barn dance celebrating the completion of a quilt she and a bevy of women—crowded close to their church's old Franklin stove—had spent winter Sunday afternoons creating. There she met Quentin Lilly, a stranger from across the river. He was a stocky red-head with light-brown eyes and an engaging smile. His attentive patience was exactly the balm she needed. He asked permission to kiss her the first time. *Asked* her. That first kiss, hidden behind a rhododendron in full bloom, was the kiss she had expected from Joseph—reserved yet tantalizing, pulsing with an undercurrent of promise. Quentin knew how to hold in his passion. It wasn't until they were married the following year that the tiger came out of his cage.

CHAPTER TWENTY-FIVE

S he was about to settle for a much-needed nap when she heard the approach of a trotting horse. She knew the rider, well before he reached the yard and dismounted. She stoked the stove fire with kindling, dropping pieces, and picked up her sewing at the table. She held the needle and cloth, as she waited for the knock, expecting to jump. Instead she heard merely a faint tap-tap-tap, hardly louder than a distant woodpecker, as if her visitor didn't wish to be heard.

Suzanne rose on uncertain legs and found the latch. There he stood, his hat in both hands, his head hunched forward with a slight tilt. He looked to her like a man expecting to be hit.

"Miss Suzanne, I don't mean to disturb you," Joseph began. "I'm just passing by. May I have a word?"

"Joseph! Whatever brings you this way? Come in and have a cup of coffee. I've just now fired the stove."

Suzanne retreated to the stove while Joseph took a seat at the table. As soon as the coffee pot was in place, she took the seat across.

"Now tell me, how is your family? I heard about your pa's passing and I was sorry to know it. How are Will and Becky?"

She was talking too fast, trying to push her way past the confusion and alarm whipping her pulse into a frenzy. Why is he here?

She saw him swallow before he spoke. "They're all right, I guess. If they don't work themselves to death. The farm's gone to Will. Becky's married with a little one. I'm taking a job with the railroad. B and O. That's why I come by. I'm heading out next week, up to Pittsburgh for now. Don't know where I'll end up."

Suzanne couldn't look at him. She wanted to reach for the shirt and needle, but remembered her clumsiness with the wood. She kept her hands clasped before her and fixed her eyes on them, a rigid little monument of sanity she could settle her rampaging thoughts upon.

"Will and Becky will miss you."

"I reckon."

Knowing it was too soon for the coffee to be hot, Suzanne rose to check it. She took a cup down from a shelf, then a small plate. With exaggerated care, she centered the cup on the plate, as if it were a saucer.

"Joseph," she said without turning toward him.

He waited.

"I'm sorry we're out of sugar and there's no more milk until tonight's milking. Will you take your coffee black?"

"Black." He nodded. She was half-turned now.

Suzanne spun back to the cupboard, pretended to be looking for the sugar she had already said was spent. Sitting back down across from Joseph felt impossible.

She seized on a topic. "You may have heard about Quentin Junior. He's fast asleep on the little tick there by the woodbox if you'd like to have a peek."

"Lordy, I walked right by him!" Joseph got up and eased, cat-like, to the woodbox. "He's sweet as a fawn, Suzanne."

Suzanne noticed the "Miss" had fallen away, and that helped somehow.

"He's a good baby, mostly. But he's teething just now and kept me up most of the night."

Joseph smiled. "That's a common complaint, I'm afraid."

A wisp of steam rose from the coffee pot, which had not cooled entirely from its morning work. Unwilling to wait for a boil, Suzanne poured the cup full and brought it to the table as Joseph joined her. Stiffly, she forced herself to sit.

Joseph, confused by the plate-cup combination, picked it up, nearly spilling his drink. Without taking a sip, he set the pair back down.

He fixed his dark eyes on Suzanne. "I oughtn't be here, but I don't want to leave without saying some things. Years back, I done you wrong, and I haven't been able to forget. I was troubled by Becky's... situation. I lost my temper."

You did?

He continued. "I said things in anger. I'll rest easier if I tell you how it preys on me. I'd like to know.... I'd like to ask, if you can forgive me for what I done."

Suzanne gaped at him. Joseph, who she'd done her best to hate for that day so clouded with shame and sorrow she couldn't bear to think of it. Her fist had broken his nose, but the first blow had been her lie. It had never occurred to her the blows had reached his heart, that he had felt the same loss to the same degree as hers. And here he sat with his face as beautiful as she remembered with its strong lines of nose and jaw, with his eyes sweet as a beagle pup's, looking like a man about ready to bust out crying, asking if she could forgive him. And the man thinly disguising the lively, good-natured boy who had been her closest friend and confidante, and the boy overwhelmed with regret.

She wanted desperately to speak, but her throat was locked up. Her brain, too, had gone into some sort of spasm of dysfunction—no coherent word arrangement was coming to order.

Suzanne rose and came around the table. Joseph stood so quickly he knocked over the chair. He caught it in time, eager not to wake the baby.

She lifted a hand, touching the side of Joseph's nose with an unsteady forefinger. She pressed her hand against his cheek to stop the shaking. "I didn't have to hit you... so hard."

Joseph's hand closed over hers. His answer was a muted croak. "I had it coming."

Frozen, Suzanne lowered her gaze to eye-level and stared at the black stubble of Joseph's shaved throat. She felt herself balancing on a fulcrum, with only a second to determine the direction of tilt. She could drop her hand and step back. She could say, "You'd best go," and he would go.

Or, she could perhaps eclipse that haunting memory....

Joseph's chin came to rest, ever so gently, on the crown of her head. As if her spirit left her body, Suzanne saw him standing with his eyes closed, absorbing what he hoped was exoneration.

Vaguely, she was aware of her habitual anger, like a wound reopened and bleeding afresh, draining from her. She was left light-headed, trying to ignore a sticky residue clining to her for tempting, for misleading, for pushing the boy into a corner until he—until they—shattered what could have been a lifelong love.

The fault was more mine than yours.

Joseph lowered his hand, and she did the same. He took the smallest of steps backward.

Move away! Suzanne told herself, but the space that had opened between them was so frigidly cavernous she reached reflexively for him, her arms closing. She let her head tilt back, her blue eyes locking on his brown.

"Joe."

Her brain formed its last lucid thought—all's lost.

Once again, Joseph made a supreme effort to show restraint, while Suzanne, having cut herself free, was the aggressor. His resistance was brief, however, and she had her way.

The baby didn't wake until they were through. Not until after Suzanne had watched Joseph ride away. She watched, stunned by what she had instigated and seen to completion. Watched, warming the lukewarm coffee in her hands, as his shoulders, the dark hair over his ears, the top of his wide-brimmed hat, dropped below her line of sight.

He never once looked back, lest she see his weeping.

It was later, while nursing her fretful baby, Suzanne realized Joseph must have passed Quentin, his two unmarried sisters, and their parents on their way to the funeral of a Lilly cousin on Bluestone River that morning. Their paths would have crossed somewhere along New River, the Lillys moving upward toward Bluestone, Joseph coming down toward Madam's Creek. Only extreme sleep deprivation had kept Suzanne from joining the family for the trip, which would occupy the entire day.

So Joseph had known she was likely alone. She couldn't help suspecting he'd come across the river on other business, but had seized the opportunity to visit when it presented itself.

She also realized she hadn't said goodbye, that once their mouths had met, they hadn't spoken another word, except for each other's names. The silence of Joseph's departure was fitting, as if they were already stepping into the void of never seeing each other again.

CHAPTER TWENTY-SIX

"Son," said Suzanne, "I can't expect you to understand. Your father was a man I grew up with. He didn't force himself on me. I want you to know that. We had... unfinished business. It was wrong, I know that. I have regret, and I've prayed for years. But what's done is done."

"Who is he?" Marcus's words were measured and crisp, like hammer blows.

Maylene could do nothing but look from one to the other. Neither would meet her gaze.

"His name was Joseph Cook. I don't know if he's dead or alive. Or where he is. He moved away before you were born. His mother was a Cherokee. He favored her and Jenny favors him. I'm 'shamed to say I never knew who fathered you until she was born. Then there was no question ."

"Who are my kin?" More hammer strikes.

"I lost touch when I left Brooks Mountain. His mama died when he was small. His pa and brother are gone now, too. He had a sister. I heard she married a hard man, a Wallace fellow, and moved up on Broomstraw. Heard he kept her home like a tethered dog. I doubt I'd know her if I saw her. It's been twenty years or more."

"Only me?"

"Yes, only you. Your pa must never know."

"He's not my pa."

Broomstraw Ridge wasn't high enough for the towering rage he felt. Despite the laboring of his heart and lungs, shirt soaked through with sweat, and leg muscles set afire, Marcus continued to Jumping Branch where he paused only long enough to cup mouthfuls of water with both hands from the stream that snaked across its modest valley. Beyond the knot of buildings that made up the rebuilt village, he tackled several hundred yards of the Turnpike, curving in indirect assault of White Oak Mountain, before dropping onto a lichen-encrusted sandstone outcrop. From his perch on the mountain's shoulder he could see a vast distance to the south, beyond Bluestone Mountain and Ellison Ridge, past Bluestone River's gorge to long, flat-topped ridges, faint and blue, marking the Virginia border.

It was a striking view, and not entirely lost on a man whose thoughts were elsewhere.

Marcus burned with all the fury he'd held at bay the past four years. The mistreatment that had ended Junior's life. His own forced service in a war he'd wanted no part of. Being wrenched away from Maylene. Johnny's death. The ache of his brothers' absence. His failed courage on the Greenbrier. His inability to put the nightmare of war behind him. The dim-wits who wouldn't let the war be over. Having to watch the father he'd always looked up to crippled by injury and whiskey. And now learning that father wasn't his father.

"God-damned sonofabitch! Jesus Christ!"

He stood up and screamed every obscenity he knew. He yelled a long, wordless shout loud enough to wake the dead. He stooped to snatch up small rocks, which he threw as far as his strength allowed, watching them disappear into the treetops below. Finally depleted, he folded into a squat and began to cry. At long last, the vessel could hold no more hurt and Marcus cried for all he'd been carrying, unable to find a way to spill it. Great wracking sobs shook his torso as he rocked, holding himself together in his own tight embrace.

It was then that a second seawall gave way and Marcus knew the full force of the enervating dread he'd never corralled since he first contemplated the possibility of being drafted. He had feared for his life. For Junior's. His father's. For Johnny's. He had feared he would have to kill. He had feared God's judgement. More than anything else, he had been continually sick with the fear he would never find his way back to Maylene. And then he had come home to find he hadn't come home to her at all, but lived like a hollowed-out husk with the new fear she had betrayed him.

Marcus shuddered with the impact of it all. But, unexpectedly, it soothed him to cry. He sat down, legs splayed before him, and let himself cry. He sat and cried until he trailed off in hiccups.

God, I'm a snotty mess.

Protecting the white shirt, Marcus wiped tears and mucus from his face with the backs of his hands. He took note of a red-tailed hawk circling in the cloudless sky, two turkey vultures hanging unsteadily in the air above it. He took note, too, of a tremor in the hand that shielded his eye against the afternoon sun.

He got up and started back down, soon stopping at Jumping Branch to wash away residues of grief. Splashing water over his tear- and sweat-streaked cheeks, he was reminded of his sisters' baptism and hoped there might be a similar cleansing of spirit in his bathing. He recognized how much lighter he felt than when he'd paused at this same spot only an hour before. He'd left some burdens on White Oak, by far the worst of which, the one flailing his soul raw, had been his rage at Maylene.

As Marcus straightened, he noticed two boys fifty yards upstream. The smaller one, who appeared no older than four or five, attempted to cross the creek on a fallen sapling. He lost his balance, and the older boy reached up from where he stood in the shallow water to grasp a forearm. Watching, Marcus felt as if a hand closed around his own left forearm, and a memory came to him. But it was a memory inverted—now it was he, not Maylene, swept downriver by a merciless current over bruising boulders. It was he who failed to find a foothold and knew the rising, thrashing panic of mortal danger. And it was Maylene who steadied him with her grip, refusing to let go at any cost.

Marcus looked down the length of his slim legs. Yes, he'd gotten upright. And, yes, he owed her.

Suzanne was out the door right behind him, evidently in no mood for further conversation. That suited Maylene. She paced the porch, back and forth, her thoughts frenzied like a dog on a fresh scent, zigzagging across the tangled brush of her brain. In the background waited a featherbed of relief, but she wouldn't settle there. Not yet.

At length, finding the porch no help, she started up the ridge, thinking to find Marcus in his usual spot, the high place he'd often retreated to for cooling off when troubled by Junior's insults, his mother's licks with a switch, or any other particularly distressing affront. Climbing steadily up the path, she watched her feet, and that helped her put her thoughts in a straighter line.

Of course her parents hadn't questioned Jenny's parentage. Maylene had come directly home to them when Marcus left that June, and soon showed signs of pregnancy. To them, Jenny was the baby God gave them. "The Lord works in mysterious ways." They simply adored their granddaughter.

The trail began making switchbacks as the slope steepened. Undeterred, Maylene considered how naïve she had been to think such acceptance would be equally simple for Marcus. The war had turned his world inside out. Father against son. Boys dying next to grandfathers. Otherwise normal men becoming demons, doing things she didn't want to know. She couldn't begin to imagine what Marcus had witnessed and endured. What he had been forced to do.

And she had expected him to have the same unshakable faith in her that her family did? When he returned home to a baby who looked like Jenny? How could she have expected him to shrug off what must have felt like a knife to his gut?

Maylene's eyes stung with tears. Why didn't I talk to him?

She realized her hesitation had been due in part to apprehension. She could hear Marcus saying, No, nothing's wrong. With Pa the way he is and Junior and Johnny gone, there's a lot on me. I get worn out. It's not like being kids anymore, Maylene. There's work waiting on me every minute.

And she could see him rising from the table to get back to that work as she felt her heart break with the realization there was no hope of things changing. She would remain lonely for her lost Marcus while the Marcus she had continued to push her away. As long as she didn't raise the topic of their alienation, she wouldn't hear those words, and she could tell herself Marcus missed their closeness as much as she did and was doing what he could to reclaim it, however slowly.

She had also feared her reaction to knowing unequivocally Marcus suspected she had been unfaithful.

Maylene's thoughts turned to her father, who had risked arrest when he helped a deserter, a total stranger.

What have I risked to heal us?

She could think of nothing, and winced inwardly at the realization she'd been too busy nursing her hurt feelings to take any bold action.

Grow up!

Breathing heavily, Maylene slowed her steps. She stopped. She then turned back, having changed her mind. She felt unready, inadequate.

Give him time to sort all this out. He'll come home when he's ready.

Back at the cabin, she considered the options of something—anything—she could do for Marcus. She would tidy up. She was swinging the door aside to reach for the broom behind it when a blemish in the lower corner of the smooth wood, next to a hinge, caught her eye. She stooped to inspect it and discovered it wasn't a blemish at all but a small heart with letters inside. She had to drop to all fours to see clearly . . . M + M.

She settled onto her folded legs and ran a finger over the heart, feeling something catch in her throat. The door, in effect, had been Marcus's wedding gift to her. It was the door that shut out well-meaning but nosy in-laws and gave them sanctuary, shutting out for a brief time even the larger world with its perpetual threat of heartbreak. They would close that door during their honeymoon week and know complete focus on each other.

It touched her that Marcus had inscribed it. M and M; there was no other pairing for either of them. She wanted their union to last until the chestnut door was warped and worn, scuffed by the feet of children and grandchildren, stained by rain and snow blown over the threshold.

She thought of Marcus shaping the door, the floor, the cabin logs with his young muscles and hopeful dreams. Wrestling each part into place. Had she ever thanked him for making their home? Had she ever thanked him for the thousands of things....

She drew in her breath, realizing. She had never thanked him for pulling her from the river that spring day, and saving her from a fatal chill in the storm that followed. Getting her safely home.

Why did I not?

She kissed a fingertip and pressed it to the center of the carved heart. She rose, then, energized with eagerness to see her man.

Don't dawdle, Marcus. Come to me.

Her energetic sweeping went quickly, and Maylene soon needed another way to pass the time. Landing on the idea of grooming Blackjack, she went to the barn for supplies, then whistled for the gelding the way Marcus did. The black horse trotted to the gate.

Maylene led him to the cabin, tied him to the porch railing, and began. She curried and brushed until Blackjack gleamed like an obsidian blade.

Marcus saw the pair as he came out of the woods beyond the pasture. Maylene, with her sleeves pushed up, had a fistful of tail in one hand, an iron comb in the other. With care, she worked knots out of the long coarse hairs, pausing to pat Blackjack's rump. The horse shimmied his skin with the landing of each fly, adeptly ejecting it, yet he welcomed Maylene's touch.

Marcus climbed over the split rails and relaxed his pace, watching. Maylene had always been good with Dolly and Spit, now with Pal and Blackjack. He liked that about her, her ease with animals. He took in her freckled arms, her golden hair pulled back, her breasts pushing against the linen bodice of her dress. There was so much to treasure about her, his Maylene. How had he allowed himself to become blind?

He felt simultaneously weak and desirous, as if drained of what had kept him upright and hungry to replace it with something else.

Maylene sensed someone looking at her and turned around. She smiled and set the comb down on the porch, gave Blackjack a final pat.

Husband of mine, it's about time.

"Don't he look prettied-up," said Marcus. "I've never gotten all the snarls out of his tail."

Maylene thought it curious the way Marcus kept one hand behind his back. "I'll turn him out."

Marcus had added a pasture gate near the cabin so she didn't have to go far. She came back to find Marcus sitting on the steps. He rose when she approached, presenting her a small bouquet of flowers—an awkward collection of Queen-Anne's lace, chicory, and wild sunflowers of varying lengths. The blossoms of Queen-Anne's lace were already beginning to curl into cups. Marcus had given her countless gleanings from his wanderings. Maylene recalled squirrels, passenger pigeons, grouse, blackberries, ramps, mushrooms, walnuts, sassafras roots for tea…. But never flowers.

"These here are for you."

For the third time that afternoon, tears blurred Maylene's vision. As she accepted the gift, she was aware of something warm and steady emanating from Marcus, like heat off Blackjack's dark, sun-baked coat. It reminded her of something.

What is it?

It came to her. It was the aspect he'd had after asking her to marry him, when that strange peacefulness had come over him. And she knew, looking up at Marcus as he stood on the step above her, so still and quiet, he had made the irrevocable turn for home.

She also knew what she wanted to give him in return.

They began gently, almost shyly, but soon crashed down on the bed in a cascade of kissing, tearing at each other's clothes, tearing at the barrier they'd built between them. They were as they had been three years before, in this same place. Could they be the same people?

It didn't take long for Marcus to climax. Maylene remained too distracted by the day's events to find release, but she took deep satisfaction in feeling and watching Marcus make that arching journey. Then they lay tangled and naked, their forceful breaths easing. Marcus kissed Maylene's eyelids, her nose, her throat. He was as tender as a mother caressing a newborn. For the first time, Maylene pressed her lips against the lumpy scar where Marcus's right eye had once rested. He didn't flinch. She held his tanned face in her hands. She traced his mouth with a forefinger. Looking into his eye, she saw the alluring mystery of dark water beneath the creek's falls and knew that as well and as long as she'd known her mate there would forever remain depths of him beyond her reach. Depths she would do them both wrong to probe.

Unwilling to let their bodies part, she slid down and rested her head on his chest, against his bearded chin.

In spite of herself, she asked. "Do you love me?"

Marcus was momentarily taken aback. Hadn't he just given his all showing her? If he hadn't been in such a state of satiated contentment, he might have felt annoyance. Women are odd creatures, he thought, smiling.

"Always," he answered, running a hand over her silky head.

Maylene kissed his neck.

"Don't forget," he added.

"I shan't."

They were quiet for a bit before Marcus said, "Do you find me hideous?"

It was Maylene's turn to be fazed. "My lord, no! Whatever would make you think so?"

"I only wondered."

"Your eye? I don't notice anymore. You are the same to me as always."

"Good." Marcus added, "Or is that good?"

"Of course."

Maylene felt strangely ill-at-ease and changed the subject. "I saw something today when I went after the broom."

"On the door?"

"Was it a secret?"

"I'd near forgotten it. I hoped you'd see it when you needed to." His torso rocked Maylene as he chuckled.

"What."

"All I could think about when I was working on the door was taking you to bed. I was sore distracted that week."

Maylene smiled. "What do you think about now?"

Marcus felt too good with a naked wife atop him to divulge the grief and harrowing memories that shadowed him. He allowed himself the luxury of a long, deep breath. "It don't seem like much has changed in that regard."

"Scoundrel."

"Temptress." He kissed the top of Maylene's head.

They were quiet again for a while, listening to the companionable chirping of a cricket that had taken up residence in their room. The steady din of outdoor crickets sounded in the distance. Otherwise, the late day was still.

Maylene felt the change in Marcus's breathing as he fell asleep, the twitch of his hand on her back. She took in his smell, pungent from his exertions but comfortingly familiar. She listened to his heartbeat and thought how grateful she was a bullet hadn't stopped it.

As fragile as birds' eggs, she thought. That's what we are.

Then the irksome thought she'd been trying to keep submerged muscled its way to the surface. Why had she never told Marcus he was good-looking until this day? She had been a vain girl hungry for flattering words and never once given a thought to his need for the same. How was he to know how she loved the sight of his strong, wide hands or the creases that formed at the sides of his mouth when he smiled? The way his hair dropped forward and grazed her face and the muscles of his shoulders and torso tensed and then began working when the love-making storm rose in him. The pride she felt knowing it was a storm she alone could calm.

I've never told him how I see him. Why?

It occurred to her with a pang of sadness she'd been denying herself, as well as Marcus, that seeing.

Maylene's pensiveness began to turn into a storm of her own brewing, and she found herself wishing her husband was awake and feeling tempestuous, too, right then. But she denied the urge to wake him.

Think of the sort of day he's had. Let the poor man rest!

"Were you fond of Amos?" Marcus asked without opening his eyes.

The question was so abrupt Maylene almost wondered if Marcus was talking in his sleep. She hadn't heard that name spoken in years.

"For about a minute."

"I didn't like him."

Maylene hoped Marcus couldn't feel the smile she was unable to stifle. "He helped me see what I had in you."

"What did he do that made you dismiss him?"

"He tried to kiss me." It was near enough to the truth, Maylene thought.

"That's it? He tried to kiss you and you sent him packing?"

"That's about it. It felt all wrong. I wanted it to be you."

"I was dreadful scared I'd lose you."

"I knew that dread when you were away." Maylene hesitated. "And afterwards."

Marcus kissed the top of her head again. "I can see that."

Maylene was nearly thrown off when Marcus rose on one elbow.

"Amos Wallace is my cousin?"

Maylene couldn't suppress a guffaw. "I wondered when you'd catch on."

"Son of a bitch," Marcus said, lying back down. "That don't rest easy with me."

"Well, he's gone and I don't see any point in bothering yourself about it."

Amos was one of the many soldiers who had simply disappeared, either by desertion or deposition in one of the countless unnamed graves the war had left in its wake.

Maylene could tell Marcus was bothering himself about it. She thought how unsettled his mother must feel, too. "You should talk to your ma."

"I know, but not just yet. She took her sweet time spilling the beans."

"She could have taken her secret to the grave."

"Seems that was her intention."

"Until Mrs. Nivens...." Maylene lifted her head, planting her chin on Marcus's breastbone. "Do you think we should thank her?"

Marcus harrumphed. "I'll thank that woman 'bout the time Hell freezes over."

"Don't it make you spitting mad?" he added.

"What Mrs. Nivens said?"

"That, too, but I was thinking about you being talked about when Mama's the one deserves it."

"I guess I hadn't thought that through."

Marcus regretted what he'd said and didn't want Maylene thinking it through. He ran a hand down her spine to the curve of a buttock. "You've put some weight back on. I'm right pleased."

"A little. We should get something to eat. We haven't had a thing since breakfast."

"I'm hungry as a spring bear."

He gnawed playfully on her shoulder, making Maylene squirm and squeal and become hopeful another hunger would overrule their appetite for food. Marcus rolled them both over and rediscovered Maylene's breasts. He nuzzled her throat with his nose.

"May?" It was his pet name for her, unused since their honeymoon.

"Marc?" She held him tightly, kissed his salty forehead.

"Can you tolerate me again?"

"Try me."

CHAPTER TWENTY-SEVEN

Suzanne had prayed long and hard the baby would be Quentin's. If not, she prayed the baby would resemble her, not Joseph, whose strong Indian features would shriek of betrayal.

Marcus came as a great relief, a near copy of herself. It was his personality that made her suspect he wasn't Quentin's. He was much more like Joseph with his quickness of mind, his boundless curiosity, his quirky creativity, and his contentment with his own contemplative company.

Suzanne felt she had piled the greater sin of adultery upon her previous sin of lies, and she expected God's wrath. She vowed to be good to Quentin, who had never done anything to deserve disloyalty, and thereafter reserved the outpourings of her temper for her children, who knew a sharp tongue and a mean switch as well as tender words and touches.

And she was good to Quentin, although he never knew the tigress Joseph encountered that summer day, the day Suzanne was unable, despite decades of self-castigation, to entirely remove from her mind. She would be caught unawares by the taste of tepid coffee, the strident cries of a killdeer, the sight of sweat trickling in front of a dark-haired man's ear—and be catapulted back to that still morning when she allowed a heady cocktail of lust, nostalgia, pity, and genuine affection to overwhelm her morality.

It surprised Suzanne the way her children thrived, and she dared hope their health was a sign of God's forgiveness. The war smashed that hope to bits, leaving Suzanne with a hollowed-out feeling. She suspected God had used her sons and husband as a means of punishing her at last, that their suffering and deaths had been her fault.

Jenny was another lash of the whip. No, you shall not forget, you shall not yet be forgiven.

Suzanne didn't crack. She prayed for Quentin and her remaining children. She cared for her husband as he sank into addiction and made no word of complaint as she took on more and more of his tasks.

The toll on her body, however, was escalating. It had been no simple thing for her small frame to bear nine children. Her bladder sagged to a position of defeat, muscles that once supported and controlled it being badly weakened. How many thousands of times had she hoisted a child onto a hip? The lifting of firewood and pails of water and milk, the demands of laundry and garden—these and a dozen other chores had rendered her nearly incontinent, and this, too, she saw as proof of God's disfavor.

By now an unguarded laugh or sneeze could spell calamity. Getting to church and back was a source of mounting anxiety. Suzanne didn't dare risk a sip on Sunday mornings, for fear of the rough ride home. She was parched and headachy by the time the house came into sight each week. Travels any farther than the church were out of the question, frequent stops were no longer safeguard enough.

She was becoming a recluse, dependent on ready access to woods or chamber pot, and wrapped in a heavy cloak of regret and shame. Her children, blaming age and fatigue, sought ways to lighten their mother's workload. Eliza and Rachel, however, were being courted, one by the pastor's nephew who was visiting from Lewisburg, the other by a Lilly second cousin. Suzanne encouraged them.

She wasn't always easy to help.

Now, this day, Marcus knew part of her shuttered pain. Suzanne felt some easing of the load for having told him, despite his reaction. If he hated her for what she'd done, she believed she deserved it.

She wore her same stoic face when Marcus appeared in the doorway, asking if there might be a bite of something to eat.

Neither spoke as Suzanne packed green beans, fried chicken, and cobs of corn. Marcus wasn't blind to her pain, but his own was still fresh, his anger unresolved. His mother could have spared him more than a year of unnecessary torment. She had torn part of his identity away—his self as a son of Quentin Lilly. Tarnished his image of her. Burdened him with a secret he must keep the rest of his life.

Thank you was not in his vocabulary this particular day.

As he left he said only, "It ain't my place to judge."

Suzanne made no reply.

CHAPTER TWENTY-EIGHT

Marcus returned from the house with a basket of leftovers in one hand and a daughter's ankle in the other. Jenny rode his shoulders, forcing him to duck to protect her head as he made his entry. Spit, he thought, would have given a little buck to swipe her off.

"Suppertime!" he announced.

Maylene had trimmed the bedraggled flowers to more-equal lengths and was arranging them in a cream pitcher. The smell of chicken fried in bacon grease made her aware of how ravenous she was.

After they ate, Maylene was clearing the table when she caught a fragrance—faint but distinctive—wafting up from within her dress.

"I smell like carrots," she said.

Marcus threw back his head and laughed at the plank ceiling. "I'd wager you do, from head to toe."

The words had no sooner left Maylene's mouth than she knew the answer. It was the smell of Queen Anne's lace—wild carrot—transferred from Marcus's hands to her skin. She gave her husband a sidelong look and grinned.

Marcus scooped up Jenny and made a rush at his wife. "Baby, your mama's a carrot and we're gonna catch her and eat her up!"

Jenny stretched her arms toward Maylene, squealing with delight. "Mama cawwot! Mama cawwot!"

"Catch her!" Marcus yelled.

Maylene screamed and ran around the table, her husband and daughter on her heels. After a few rounds, she was dizzy and let Jenny's hands reach her dress.

"I catched her, Papa!"

Marcus closed the gap and snared them both in a hug. He play-nibbled on Maylene's neck, then Jenny's. Jenny convulsed with giggles and Maylene laughed until she had to brush away tears. How many could she produce in a single day?

Marcus carried Jenny to the rocker by the hearth, and placed her on his lap. "Your papa's gonna rob the bees and get some honey tomorrow. Honey for my honey-child."

At that moment, watching them, Maylene's mouth dropped open, ripe with news. She had to stop herself from saying there would be a baby in the spring. She was as sure as she was that the sun was setting, sending a narrow beacon of light onto the chimney stones. But she told herself to wait, there was time. It occurred to her that time was finally their ally. It had tick-tocked agonizingly while Marcus was away and had continued to stall as she waited for the full Marcus to return. Now, she welcomed its ponderous beat. Marcus could have eternity if he needed it to come completely back to himself. She would luxuriate in every sweet minute. There was all the time in the world to tell him he would be a father again.

Marcus rocked with Jenny, thinking how wonderfully unaffected she was by her parents' tension, by his standoffishness. She had so many loving aunts and uncles and grandparents, what did it matter if her parents were a bit off kilter? And she had never known unkindness. By all appearances, she was a bubbly two-year-old, full of questions, free of care.

He thought he would rock her to sleep. He was drowsy himself, limp with fatigue. He realized the weight of it then, slowly rocking, the weight of battling not only the Union for three years but himself. So much that had been required of him—violence, scheming, thievery, deception—was contrary to his nature it had exhausted him near to death to play his role. He had since wearied himself with the exertion of holding Maylene at arms' length, the self-denial of refusing to be a child again with Jenny. His entire life, up until his homecoming, being close to Maylene had required no effort whatsoever. It had been a searing strain denying what was as much a part of him as his own skin. And the reason had been nothing but cowardice. He hadn't seen it that way until now. With fear masquerading as anger, suspicion, numbness… how was he to get a clean shot at it? It struck him that his dread of the most agonizing wound to the heart had come close to costing him—them—everything, sealing off his heart for good.

Rocking, rocking, he let his head fall back against the smooth wood. A prayer welled up in him. Lord, knead the knots out of me, and help me ease up and do what comes natural. Help me do right by Maylene and Jenny.

He added, My wife and my little child, as if fearful it had been so long since God had heard from him He might need clarification.

Jenny squirmed. "Papa?"

"Jenny?"

"Play horsey?"

"No, Jenny-bear, it's late for that. And your papa's wore out. We can blame your mama for that."

His attempt to give his wife a stern look was such a comical failure that Maylene's inner hummingbird returned as a rooster flapping vigorously at dawn. If Marcus's lap hadn't been occupied, she might have taken flight and landed there.

"I'll tell you a story instead," Marcus said.

Jenny twisted her head around and looked at her father, as if to be sure he was going to deliver, before settling back against him.

Maylene pulled a chair close. It had been a long time.

Marcus began. "There was a wild black stallion, as tall as Pal. He lived in a cave at the base of a cliff, way high up on top of a mountain...."

Maylene closed her eyes. As the story continued, she could see sunlight dappling a sand spit along Madam's Creek, Marcus squatting, drawing with a birch twig.

"The stallion guarded the cave, allowing only children to enter. There was a magical world inside, but the secret way in was to be asleep and go there in dreams...."

Maylene felt cool, gritty mud between her toes. She sensed the nearness of a boy whose lively mind and generous heart formed the bedrock of her world.

"When they passed through the fog curtain, what do you think they saw when they stepped into the cave?" Marcus whispered into Jenny's ear.

But Jenny was slipping into her own dreams. As her eyes closed, Maylene's opened. "You're making this up as you go, aren't you."

"Is there any other way?"

And he winked at her with his deep brown eye, over the head of glossy black hair resting against his chest, the sleepy head of his very own baby daughter.

ACKNOWLEDGEMENTS

I would like to thank the following people for their invaluable help. Jessie Reeder, who generously took time from her own research and writing to provide extensive editorial assistance, sage advice, photo editing, and encouragement. Bev Wright, a direct descendent of Jefferson Bennett, who supplied information and joined me in exploration of literature and graveyards, as well as read the manuscript in draft form and provided commentary and unwavering support. Employees of New River Gorge National River, who directed me to various historic sites. Staff of the Summers County Library, who assisted with historic research. Writers Paul Dodd and Phyllis Campbell Whitley and historian Wayne Harvey, whose expertise was helpful. Jon Averell, whose docudrama, "Passing Through Sandstone," offered much useful information. Nancy Hopps, who listened with her characteristic patience and interest to my ups and downs as the book-birthing process unfolded, and who also offered photographic assistance. Cynthia Lenhart for unceasingly prodding me, with humor and love, to manifest my heart's desires. Wendy Dingwall and Linda Sack of Canterbury House Publishing, for their adept professionalism, patience with my questions, and willingness to back a fledgling author. As well as my cousin Steve, who personified persistence in the early years of his writing career. And for this warm-hearted New River community that honors those who came before.

ABOUT THE AUTHOR

Photo credit: Nancy Hopps

Betsy Reeder grew up in then-rural Maryland and later found her way to Central Appalachia, where she works as a writer and biologist. Her avocations include walking, birding, haphazard gardening, creative writing, political activism, volunteerism, spiritual exploration, natural history, local history, captivating novels, music, animals (both wild and tame), and every second spent with family and friends. She is especially grateful to have realized her long-held dream of a home in the mountains.

OTHER BOOKS BY ELIZABETH REEDER

Cowgirl Dreams Elizabeth Easley 2000
Heartwood: A Journal of Nature and Soul, 2006
Birds Nearby, 2009 (A children's book)

ESSAY

Bastion in the anthology *What Does it Mean to be White in America?*

CPSIA information can be obtained
at www.ICGtesting.com
Printed in the USA
FFHW021618160319
51077032-56478FF